THE LIMIT

THE
LIMIT

BY KRISTEN LANDON

Aladdin
NEW YORK   LONDON   TORONTO   SYDNEY

ALADDIN

An imprint of Simon & Schuster Children's Publishing Division

1230 Avenue of the Americas, New York, NY 10020

First Aladdin hardcover edition September 2010

Copyright © 2010 by Kristen Landon

For information about special discounts for bulk purchases, please contact Simon & Schuster Special Sales at 1-866-506-1949 or business@simonandschuster.com.

The Simon & Schuster Speakers Bureau can bring authors to your live event. For more information or to book an event contact the Simon & Schuster Speakers Bureau at 1-866-248-3049 or visit our website at www.simonspeakers.com.

The text of this book was set in Janson Text.

Manufactured in the United States of America 0710 OFF

2 4 6 8 10 9 7 5 3 1

Library of Congress Cataloging-in-Publication Data

Landon, Kristen, 1966–

The limit / Kristen Landon. — 1st Aladdin hardcover ed.

p. cm.

Summary: When his family exceeds its legal debt limit, thirteen-year-old Matt is sent to the Federal Debt Rehabilitation Agency workhouse, where he discovers illicit activities are being carried out using the children who have been placed there.

ISBN 978-1-4424-0271-3 (hardcover)

[1. Conspiracies—Fiction. 2. Science fiction.] I. Title.

PZ7.L2317348Li 2010   [Fic]—dc22   2010012707

ISBN 978-1-4424-0273-7 (eBook)

For Von.
You would make the top floor for sure!

and

In loving memory, to one of my biggest cheerleaders,
Jenny Landon.
I miss you, my sister and friend.

ACKNOWLEDGMENTS

A huge thank-you has to go to my agent, Steven Chudney, for being the first to believe in this book and in me. You did a fabulous job pushing me to take this book to a higher level.

I also must thank my writing pals: Karlene Browning, Chris Minch, Sheila Nielson, Melissa Ochsenhirt, and Andy Spackman. Your help and insight is always superb. Many thanks also go to Deborah Halverson for her ideas, which vastly improved this book.

Also to JoAnne and Zach Colemere, and Von and Carter Landon for reading early drafts.

To all other members of my family and to my many friends for their support, interest, and positive energy— with a special thank-you to the group who double checked my math.

And, finally, to my fabulous editor, Liesa Abrams, for her incredible editorial skill, humor, and enthusiasm.

THE LIMIT

CHAPTER 01

AN EIGHTH-GRADE GIRL WAS TAKEN today.

Whispers and text messages flew through Grover Middle School. *They slapped handcuffs on her and shoved her into the back of a van. They shot her with a tranquilizer dart in the middle of the lunchroom. She escaped and she's hiding in the library—right now—texting her friends.*

The girl went to Lakeview Middle School. My cousin goes to Lakeview. He said they called her out of first period and she never came back. An eighth grader! Nobody could believe it. Up until now they'd only taken high school students.

Up until now we thought we were off-limits.

Bam-swish. Bounce, bounce. Bam-swish.

My hand—with the follow-through fingers bent— hung high in the air. "Yeah, baby, who's the free-throw king?"

"Four in a row. Big deal." Brennan stretched those

long arms of his toward the basketball and me. "Give it here."

"Why?" I asked.

"I'm gonna show you up."

"No way. I'm in the middle of a streak. Besides, you couldn't make two free throws in a row if your perfect GPA depended on it."

"Well, it doesn't, Mr. 3.997."

Ouch. Just because he never had Ms. Tullidge for English and her *You must support your thesis statement with facts*. And *Yes, Matt, ninety-three percent is* still *an A-minus in my class*.

"Taking your shooting history over the past seventeen minutes into account, the probability that you will successfully complete the next shot is only eight-point-seven percent," said Lester, who'd been standing in the same spot since my mother kicked us off the computer and made us *go outside and process some fresh air through your lungs, boys*.

Even during a basketball game Brennan and Lester processed more numbers through their brains than air through their lungs. I probably did too.

"Okay, here's what we're going to do." I slammed the ball against the concrete of my driveway with every couple of words I spoke. "Anyone who gets their hands on the ball can shoot, but we're going to score it different. We all start with . . ." Today was March 12. "Twelve points." A car drove by. It had two eights on its license plate. "Every time you score, you get to multiply by eight. Every time you miss, you have to divide by four." No reason for the four. I just pulled it out of the air. "First guy to a billion wins."

"Too easy," said Lester. "Four, eight, and twelve? Couldn't you have thrown in a three or a seven to make it more challenging?"

"The basket is going to be your challenge, runt." I only had a couple of inches on Lester, but that was enough.

"I think it's the shoes," he said, not afraid to poke fun at himself. "If I just had a pair of JockAirs, I'd score every time—according to their commercials."

"Got that right." Brennan laughed. "I'll get a pair too and join the basketball team."

I added in some fancy double-time dribbling. "Seriously, Lester, you could use a new pair of shoes. Look at those things on your feet. The stitching's coming undone."

"They're okay. They'll last a while longer."

"Why should they?" I dribbled fast and close to the ground. "You know what brand is really sweet? Keetos."

"Keetos? They cost . . . a lot."

"Yeah? So? They're cool."

3

Whistling softly, he shook his head. "Extremely expensive."

"What does it matter, if that's what you really want?" My dribbling slowed. "It just goes on your family's account."

"It matters," he said in almost a whisper. "*The limit.* Forget it. Can we just play?"

"Sure. Ready, set, go!" I faked a break to the right, leaving Lester off balance. As I sprinted for the basket, Brennan stretched up tall in front of me with that amazing reach of his that makes basketball coaches drool all over their sneakers—until they see him play. As I ducked and darted around my beanpole buddy, he twisted, trying to follow my move. His legs didn't respond fast enough, and by the time I banked the ball for an easy layup, he had one hand on the ground to break his fall.

I grabbed the loose ball and headed for the back of the driveway—just to give them a chance. "Twelve times eight. Ninety-six."

Seven more made shots with two misses thrown in got me to 12,582,912. Brennan had achieved a whopping score of 1.5. Lester hung steady at twelve.

I dribbled close to the ground, tormenting my buddies for a few more seconds. "Three more to go, boys, and there's nothing you weenies can do to stop me."

"Six by my calculations." Lester crinkled his nose

under his glasses as he squinted into the sun.

The ball froze between my palms. "What kindergarten calculations would those be?"

"I told you—four, eight, and twelve are too factorially compatible. In my mind I've been multiplying by five instead of eight—to spice things up with a few decimal points. According to my scoring system you need six more baskets."

"Can you believe this math geek?" I asked Brennan, shifting the ball from one hand to the other.

"I've been multiplying by three-point-five." He lunged for the ball, which I easily diverted with a quick dribble behind my back. Breathing heavily, he stared down at me, his hands on his hips. "According to me, you need nine more baskets."

"Geez, thanks for your input. Doesn't matter. Nine, five, twenty. I'm still skunking you two."

As I visualized the trajectory of my next shot, a car horn blasted from a few houses down the street. The honking continued every four seconds until Dad pulled into the driveway, scattering the three of us.

The guys salivated as Dad's sleek silver machine glided by us and into the garage. They continued to stare until Dad climbed out of his car and popped the trunk.

"Hey, Matt. Hello, boys."

"Hi, Mr. Dunston," said Lester.

Brennan only managed a sort of grunt.

"Been slaving at the computer all day?" I asked with a joking smile. The khaki pants and gray, blue, and pink argyle sweater-vest he wore made up his official golf uniform.

"Some days I wish," he said, shaking his head. Edging back onto the concrete, I started dribbling again. Brennan waved his long arms frantically in front of my face. Lester shuffled around under the basket. Out of the corner of my eye I noticed Dad pause, his golf clubs halfway out of the trunk, to study a small piece of paper.

"No, that wasn't right. I swear I shot a birdie on the fourth hole *and* the thirteenth." Dad's mumblings grew louder and more animated by the second, soon drowning out the thump of basketball against cement. "An eagle on the eighth? I don't think so, Miller, you cheating maggot. Ha! Par on the fifteenth. More like double bogie, with that sand trap."

My shot fell short, and Brennan easily scooped up the rebound.

"Dad? Everything okay?"

A wide, toothy grin flashed up at me. "Sure. No problems. I just let Miller cheat me out of a few th . . . ah, a few bucks." The smile stayed frozen in place as Dad neatly folded the paper and slid it into his back pocket. In one swift movement he spun around, snatched a loose golf ball from the trunk, and chucked it somewhere back in the garage. A clattering, crashing noise made Brennan stumble over his approach to the basket.

He lowered his arms and sent the basketball my way in a wimpy bounce pass. "You know what? I think I'm going to go home. It's getting close to dinner."

"Yeah, me too," said Lester, moving faster than he had all day on the court.

"Okay, see you guys later."

They'd hustled to the end of the block by the time I'd missed my way down to 768 points. Finally, I gave up and went inside, using the front door instead of going through the garage.

I headed straight for the kitchen, where a hearty aroma *should* have clued me in to what we'd soon be eating. I didn't notice one today. Before I had the chance to open the fridge for some juice, Mom stopped me.

"Wash," she said without turning around. The swoosh of her butcher knife slicing through celery stalks increased to hammering bangs.

"Ease up," I said, flicking a bit of the water from my hands against the back of her neck. "What'd the celery ever do to you?"

She kept banging, harder and faster, until she reached the end of her stalk.

"I just don't know what to do with you, Matt."

"Um . . . buy me a car like Dad's in three years for my sixteenth birthday?" I offered.

"I'm serious." She turned around, that knife in her hand looking a little too much like a weapon. "Do you have any idea who I just got off the phone with?"

Of course I didn't, so I didn't bother answering. I don't think she expected me to.

"Mr. Lochee."

"Oh."

"And *do* you have a reasonable explanation for why you stopped doing your assignments in his class?"

"Yeah."

She opened her eyes wider, even as they shot laser beams at me. The knuckles of her hand clutching the knife turned white.

"I figured it out a couple weeks ago." My words came out fast. "I had one hundred sixty-eight percent in his class. Even if I don't turn in another assignment for the rest of the semester, I'll still get a strong A-plus."

She clicked her tongue. "How can you possibly have one hundred sixty-eight percent?"

"Ask Lochee," I said, making my voice all innocent. "All I know is what I saw in his online grade book. It's not my fault if my assignments are so brilliant he can't stop himself from dumping a ton of extra-credit points into my total."

"Matt." Shaking her head, Mom twisted her mouth to hide her growing smile. She tossed the knife into the sink and grabbed me by the shoulders. The shake she gave me was more a hug than an act of aggression. "Okay, listen. Schoolwork is about more than grades. You need to do the work to learn the material, not just to maintain a 4.0."

3.997, but who wanted to get picky?

Abbie walked into the kitchen. "I'm hungry."

"You," I said, twisting to point at her. "If you finished all your work in kindergarten, would you do extra work, or would you go play?"

"Play," she said, as if the answer were so obvious the question shouldn't have been asked.

"See?" I said to Mom.

My other younger sister, Lauren, wandered in, her eyes stuck on her cell phone. "When's dinner?"

"Soon," said Mom, slipping on a pair of oven mitts.

The second she pulled open the oven door, she growled and leaned so far inside I thought the layers of makeup on her face would melt off and drip into the food. She shook the oven mitts onto the floor and grabbed the rack.

"Mom!" I yelled.

Grimacing, she slid her hands along the inside oven wall. "Lauren, run in the garage and get your father.

Now!" Lauren bolted as Mom plastered her palm against the roasting pan.

"Mom," I said, "stop touching that!"

A minute later Dad bounced into the kitchen, carrying a giggling Lauren over his shoulder. He slid her to the ground the instant his eyes landed on Mom.

"It's cold," she snapped. "Ice cold."

He reached for the door of the cupboard that contained our stash of chips and crackers. "So call a repairman."

"And have it break again in a week? No thank you. We're buying a new oven, and this time we're not going the frugal route. I'm getting every feature that's available—just like the model Wendy Beil bought last month."

"Anything you want, love." Dad blew her a kiss, poked me in the ribs, and said softly in my ear, "If a new oven's what it takes to bribe your mom into putting on a killer dinner for the Duprees, then that's what we'll have to buy her." He spoke louder, so Mom could hear. "Order it right away, honey. We're going to nail that Dupree account. Matt, start shopping for a new bike."

"But I just got—"

He wasn't listening.

"Lauren, what do you want, baby? A new phone?"

"Okay," she said, her thumbs going crazy on her current one.

"Can I have a pony?" asked Abbie.

"Absolutely." Dad rubbed his hands together. "I'm going to buy a set of custom titanium golf clubs and finally step up to a country club membership."

"Will!"

"I'll buy you anything you want too, Becca." Dad blew her another kiss. He pumped his fists and shook his hips in a weird, embarrassing, grown-up-person sort of dance as he headed for his room to change out of his golf uniform.

Ten minutes later the five of us sat around the table over bowls of freshly nuked frozen stew. Bored, Dad turned the conversation away from Abbie's description of her day in kindergarten.

"So, what's the news from middle school? Anything as exciting as a boy bringing his dead pet cricket for show and tell?"

I let out a snort. "Hardly. Middle school puts me to sleep."

"What about that girl they snatched?" Lauren asked.

Mom dunked a corner of bread into the juices of her stew. "Who snatched what girl? Did the police come? I'm surprised I didn't hear about this."

"She wasn't kidnapped. I don't know *who* took her," said Lauren, chatting away as calmly as if discussing how one of her little twelve-year-old friends had a crush on a certain boy that week. "Those people who take kids whose families go over their limit came and got her."

Dad's fork clattered to the table. "Is this true, Matt? They took a kid from middle school?"

"I guess," I mumbled. Stupid Lauren. I wish she'd think before she talked. Dad was sure to start fuming about our overreaching, too-powerful government, blah, blah, blah.

"Middle school kids." Dad shook his head. A second later his fist came down hard against the table, making a splatter of milk fly out of his glass. The rest of us jumped. "I knew it. They suck us into a bad idea—make us accept it—and then crank up the rottenness another couple of notches. It's only been what—two years since they started this workhouse program?"

"A year and a half," Mom corrected.

"Either way, not long at all," said Dad. "The whole stinking program is just going to get worse and worse." Dad flung his napkin onto the table. A corner of the white fabric landed in his bowl, soaking up the brown liquid.

Mom took another careful bite of stew and lowered her fork slowly to the table. "I just can't imagine any parent choosing to send one of their children to that place. What's the name of the family the girl came from?"

"I don't know," said Lauren. "She went to Lakeview.

Goes. She *goes* to Lakeview. At least she will again when they let her come back. The kids are supposed to come back someday, aren't they? I mean, we've never known anyone who's come back, but we've also never known anyone who got taken. They really don't take many kids there, do they." *Stupid, stupid Lauren. Dinner isn't supposed to be so tense. Can we just drop this subject?* "I wish we did know someone. I'd love to find out what goes on inside those workhouses."

"No you wouldn't," I said. No one really knew, of course, besides the families who'd been directly affected—and I didn't think it was a subject they loved to brag about. I could sure imagine what went on inside the workhouses.

"Did you say the girl went to Lakeview? That would explain it, then." Mom dug into her stew. "Those people who live in the Lakeview boundaries haven't got the sense of a donkey. We can't expect them to be able to manage their accounts. I suppose the government had no choice but to step in. Honey, will you please pass me the pepper?"

CHAPTER 02

"I SWEAR SOMEDAY SHE'S GOING to . . . where *is* that key?" Mom dug deep into her duffel-bag-size lime-green purse while my sisters and I waited on the porch in front of our grandmother's house. Mom ended up dumping the contents of her purse onto the padded seat of a wicker chair before she spied the elusive key to let us in. "Mother? Where are you?"

"Rebecca, is that you? I'm in the living room."

"I'm here too, Nana."

"Me too!"

"Matt and Abigail came too! What did I do to deserve such a plethora of visitors?"

Mom paused in the wide opening to the living room, slamming one high-heeled shoe into the hard-wood floor as she jammed her hands against her waist. "You tripped over that mutt of yours and nearly killed yourself, Mother. That's what you did."

"Phsssh," said Nana, waving her off. "Oh, Lauren came along as well. How nice."

"Hi, Nana," said Lauren, not bothering to glance up from her phone. "I hope your ankle doesn't hurt too much."

"It will be fine. Eventually." Nana lay lengthwise on the sofa. When she tried to push herself up, a sharp grimace twisted her face.

"You are not all right," said Mom, hustling across the room. "Let me get a look at that leg."

An insistent yipping came from farther back in the house. The guilty mutt.

"Poor Buffy. Matt, would you mind taking her out to the backyard? It's so hard for me with this"—Nana flicked her hand toward her ankle—"inconvenience."

"Inconvenience?" Mom's voice quickly reached the high, shrill level saved especially for times of stress. "You haven't even begun to think this through, have you?"

"Don't worry about it, Nana." I hustled into the kitchen. The little ball of white fluff that was Buffy bounced around in front of the wide glass door like a rubber ball while emitting high-pitched barks that sounded like a hinge in desperate need of a good oiling. As soon as I slid the door open a couple of inches, she squeezed through and raced circles around the backyard. I followed with much less enthusiasm.

Hunching under my jacket against a sharp breeze, I waited while Buffy did her thing. I'd just picked up a stick for her to chase when Lauren and Abbie joined me.

"They're fighting," said Abbie.

"Annoying," said Lauren with an eye roll and slight twitch of her head. Her hands were shoved into the pockets of her hoodie—resting her thumbs for once.

Abbie's eyes sparkled as she skipped across the back porch. "Where's Buffy?"

We played with the dog for a few minutes—until a biting wind forced us back inside.

Insistent voices carried loud and strong into the kitchen. Lauren stuck in her earbuds, pulled out her phone, and plopped into a chair at the table. Abbie let herself get absorbed with Buffy. I decided Nana needed a glass of milk, so I poured one and took it in to her.

"I'm not backing down, Mother. You're going to the hospital."

Nana smiled as she reached for the glass. "Thank you, Matt. You're so thoughtful."

"Matt, go find a pair of Nana's shoes. We're taking her to the emergency room right now."

"Sit down, Matt."

I plopped next to Mom on the big ottoman in front of the sofa. "Rebecca, you and your children are free to go wherever you want, but I'm staying right here—in my home."

"Your ankle could very well be broken." Mom

slapped the back of her hand against my shoulder. "Tell her, Matt."

I made my voice come out high and animated. "It very well could be broken." I flipped long imaginary hair over my shoulder.

"You've got her down!" Nana pounded her good leg as she chortled.

Mom slapped me again. "Stop it. This is serious." Her laughter weakened her words. "No, listen. Mother, what if something is seriously wrong with your ankle?"

"What if it isn't?" Nana thrust her chin into the air. "Then I will have given up everything for nothing." She shook her finger in Mom's face. "You know exactly what will happen if I let you take me to the hospital. They'll stamp my charts with a big, red 'Unfit to Care for Self' label and cart me off to the home for the dead and dying."

What? No. They wouldn't take Nana away. People were supposed to be sucking in their last breaths before they had to go there. At least that's what I'd always thought.

"They're called residences for the advanced in years, Mother. They're very nice institutions."

The home for the dead and dying is what I've always heard it called—unofficially of course.

"Hrmph!" Nana turned her face to the wall.

Mom leaned forward to stroke her arm. "You don't know for sure that they will classify you as unfit. This is just a temporary injury."

"Are you living with a sack over your head?" Nana shot back, jerking her arm away from Mom's touch. "They jump on any little excuse they can find. Those government people can't wait to haul off one more aging person and tuck us away in some little rat hole so they can claim our homes and all our property. Well, I'm not ready to give in. Not yet. Not without a fight."

Yeah, you go, Nana!

Mom let out a long sigh. "You know they don't claim *all* your property. You get to take your sentimental items with you. Then they sell what's left to pay your expenses at the residence. It's a fine, fair program that works well for the aging in our society."

Nana's eyes narrowed. "You've bought into all that PR they bombard us with, haven't you? I haven't. Besides, they don't allow pets."

"Well, you can't stay here alone."

"Why don't you come to our house?" I asked. "Abbie would love to camp out on Lauren's floor, and you can have her room."

"I'd love to, Matt. That's very kind of you to sacrifice your sister's room for me." She gave me a wink. "I just couldn't, though. I have to think of Buffy."

No brainer. "Bring her."

"Dad's allergies," Mom said, poking my arm.

"Oh, yeah." *Okay then, here's the plan. I'll smuggle Buffy out of here when we go to the hospital and hide her at either Brennan or Lester's house. As soon as Nana is settled in the home for the dead and dying, I'll sneak the little fur ball into her room. Nana will either keep hiding the dog with her or blow her cover and get herself kicked out of the home. Either way works.*

Mom squared her shoulders as she sat up tall on the ottoman. "I suppose there's nothing to do but move myself in with you for a while. They can't force you to move if I'm here to care for you."

I guess that could work too.

"Would you really, Rebecca? That would be wonderful."

"I'll do it as long as you agree to let me take you in to get that ankle treated first. You shouldn't need my help here for more than a week, I'd think."

"Hang on," I said. "What about us?"

"For heaven's sake, Matt. You kids are old enough to look after yourselves for a few hours after school until your father gets home from work. Any of you are capable of ordering takeout. You won't be missing out on any great home-cooked meals anyway, since I can't cook any until the new stove is delivered."

Hmm. A few days without Mom making sure I ate my whole grains and limiting my computer time. That could work out just fine, but shoot, I really *had* wanted to try the Buffy smuggling plan—just to see if I could pull it off. Putting my brains up against a government agency would've been an awesome challenge. I bet I would have won.

CHAPTER 03

"WOULD YOU LOOK AT THESE LINES?" Mom grumbled. "I really don't have the patience for this today."

"This is nothing. Just think how much longer you're going to have to wait when you take Nana to the hospital." I could joke about it because I knew Mom was going to drop us kids off at home after this trip to the store. We'd get to zone out with the TV or computer while she packed some clothes and some of the food we were buying and headed back to Nana's and then to the emergency room. "I'm going to the magazine rack."

"Fine." Mom nodded to me as she swiveled her overflowing cart into a line she found acceptable. A box with three big scented candles in glass jars slipped off the top. She grabbed it. Leave it to Mom to find a store full of things she thought she'd die without—a digital meat thermometer, throw pillows for the family-room sofa, a foot massager. All we'd come in for were crutches, a few groceries for Nana, and some frozen meals for the rest of us.

Scooting sideways, I squeezed past the lady at the front of the checkout line. Her backside bumped into me as she leaned forward for the laser eye scan that would access her account to pay the store.

"Sorry," I mumbled as I hustled away to snatch up the latest issue of *COMP*—a pretty decent computer and technology magazine.

Mom stood third in line. She opened a bottle of bubbles she'd picked up in the toy department and blew a few for Abbie to pop. Lauren, shaking her head, pretended not to be associated with either of them as her thumbs worked her phone.

I flipped through the magazine. "Today's New Digital Animation." Nothing new there. "How to Change Your Cursor." How could these people possibly think they were cutting edge? Wait. Here was something interesting. "A Techie's Dream Room Makeover."

Halfway through the article, I glanced over the top of the magazine rack that stretched along the end of the checkout counter. Mom looked down the conveyor belt, where dozens of items were creeping toward me like an endless invasion of army ants. She caught my eye and winked. I went back to the article.

Oh, yeah. This high-fidelity canopy bed had just turned into a must-have. Imagine surfing the web and watching movies while lying flat in the comfort of my own bed. No one else at school had anything like it. *Note to self—hit Dad up for one later tonight.* Once I showed it to him, he'd want one for himself as well. We'd have to get two.

I'd moved on to the description of high-tech bathroom windows when I heard a sharp gasp from Mom's checkout worker. My eyes shot up. Checkout Lady had her hand over her mouth. Mom seemed unflustered. Checkout Lady must have made a mistake. I kept reading. Hmm, electrical impulses in the glass and a liquid crystal layer to cloud up for privacy. Cool.

The usual noise and confusion of the megastore around me dimmed. It was like it faded to almost nothing, leaving only the voices of my mom and Checkout Lady. Even Abbie put a lid on her usual nonstop chatter and stuck her thumb in her mouth. I thought she'd stopped sucking her thumb a long time ago.

"I'm sure it's a mistake," Mom said. "A computer glitch somewhere."

Checkout Lady punched a few buttons on her computer while her front teeth gnawed her lower lip like a beaver working a tree. "I'm so sorry. It's not a mistake. You're over your limit."

An electric current zapped through me. No. Wait. Stuff like this didn't happen to *our* family.

"It can't be," said Mom. She flipped back her dark

23

hair in that way that made her appear confident and in control, but she couldn't hold her eyes still. Her voice dropped a couple of notches. "How is that possible?"

Abbie sucked harder on her thumb, a ring of drool building up around the edge. Lowering her phone, Lauren slunk backward, away from Mom. I still held the issue of *COMP*, but the words and pictures blurred.

"Take it back." Mom's words came out in a rush. She pulled a white plastic shopping bag out of her cart and turned it upside down, spewing the contents onto the conveyor belt. "Take it all off my account right now."

Lauren appeared by my side. She grabbed my elbow and hung on as tight as if it were a life preserver.

"I'm sorry, ma'am," said Checkout Lady. "Once you go over your limit, I'm locked out of the system until we receive clearance from the government." She pushed a few buttons on her console and raised her hands in defeat.

"Is this going to take long?" the next man in line asked.

"A few more minutes, at least," said Checkout Lady.

The man let out a grunt. "You'd think grown people would be able to manage their accounts." He snatched up the gallon of milk he'd set on the conveyor belt and walked away to find another line.

24 The next lady banged into the display rack as she

tried to maneuver her cart backward. "Stay home and stop shopping if you think you're getting close to your limit," she snapped at Mom. "It doesn't take a college degree to figure that out."

Mom stared straight ahead. Her lips trembled. Part of me wanted to follow those people and yell at them that they couldn't talk to my mother that way. A bigger part needed to stay right where I was and find out what would happen next.

"Don't you worry, ma'am," said Checkout Lady. "People always act like they've been robbed when they have to wait five minutes longer than they thought. Don't take it personally."

A sharp, metallic tune made Mom jump. She dug into her purse and pulled out her phone.

"Hello?" Her eyes got big. "Yes, it is. Listen to me. There must be some mistake. My husband said a deposit . . ." Mom's voice trailed off, and her cheeks flushed red. "It's an automated message," she said in an unsettled voice to Checkout Lady.

Mom listened silently for a few minutes, taking in quick, shallow breaths. All the color drained from her face. "I need to talk to someone," she said into the phone. Frantically, she pounded some of the buttons. "Let me talk to a real person!"

The pages of *COMP* wrinkled in my grip. 25

Lauren clamped down tighter on my arm.

"It's okay," I told her. I'm such a liar.

Mom's head jerked back an inch, and she lowered the phone. She'd been disconnected.

"I'm sorry, ma'am," said Checkout Lady. "Is there anything I can do?"

Mom sniffed and shook her head. She glanced at me. Checkout Lady, gnawing on her lip again, turned to follow her gaze. When they saw me looking back, they quickly turned away. *What? I didn't have anything more to do with this than the girls. Why single me out?* The crackers I'd eaten in the car on the way to the store turned to rocks in my stomach.

Grabbing Abbie around the wrist, Mom scurried around her shopping cart. "We're getting out of here." She snatched up Lauren's arm as well and dragged her along behind her. Mom couldn't have walked any faster without breaking into a run.

"What about my bubbles?" asked Abbie, reaching backward.

I took a look at the cart, which bulged with shopping bags. Just a few seconds ago we'd thought we desperately needed every single item in there. Now all I could think was how those unnecessary purchases had put us over the limit.

LAUREN WRENCHED HER ARM FREE
before we left the store. Mom walked
through the parking lot so fast Abbie
couldn't keep up. Mom didn't even notice
when Abbie's arm slipped out of her fingers. I scooped
up my little sister and slung her around to ride piggy-
back on me.

"Who called you?" I asked Mom. She stood by our
car urging us forward with frantic waves of her hand.
"What did they say?"

"Get in," she said, pressing the keyless entry button. "Quickly."

What? Were we bank robbers now, making our
getaway?

I slid Abbie into the backseat and climbed in the
front. Mom didn't wait for us to fasten our seat belts
before she ripped out of the parking space. I hadn't
even closed my door.

Mom reached inside her purse with one hand,
steering with the other as she zoomed through the

parking lot. She yanked out her cell phone at the same moment she pulled onto the road. A car screeched and swerved to avoid hitting us. A loud horn blast bawled us out. Mom didn't even blink.

"Slow down," I said, looking over my shoulder to make sure Lauren and Abbie had buckled their seat belts.

"Where are we going?" asked Lauren, noticing—as I did—that we were headed in the opposite direction from our house. We weren't driving toward Nana's house either.

Mom's trembling fingers struggled to dial her phone.

"Here, I'll do it," I said, taking it from her. "Who called you earlier?"

Mom opened her mouth, as if to say something, then closed it again, shaking her head.

"It was about the limit, wasn't it? Someone called because we went over. There are lots of options for people who go over, right?" I couldn't control my voice, and it got high and a little squeaky. "Supervised spending can't be as bad as everyone says."

She couldn't even look at me. "Call your father." Her voice shook as much as her fingers.

I tried Dad's office and got a busy signal. He didn't answer his cell phone.

"That probably means he's golfing," I said to Mom. "He always turns off his phone when he golfs."

"I need him," she said.

"Maybe he's golfing with Mr. Dupree right now," I said, trying to make myself feel better. "Maybe he'll land that project today. He'll get so much money we'll laugh about going over the limit. By tomorrow it won't even matter."

Mom looked at me. As she tried to smile, she choked on a sob.

Don't cry, Mom. Just tell me that everything's going to be all right. Please!

"Are we going to Dad's office?" asked Lauren. "Will he fix what's wrong?"

That must've been where Mom was headed. I couldn't think of a single other place in this section of town where we'd want to go. Mom wiped a tear from under her eyes every few seconds and drove, both hands clutched high on the steering wheel until we pulled into the parking lot of Dad's office. She stopped in one of the handicapped spaces near the front door.

"Stay here," she ordered the three of us as she jumped out of the car. She didn't bother to close the door behind her. I'd never seen Mom run in her jeans and heels before. She could go fast.

A sob came from the backseat. I looked over my shoulder. Abbie had stuck her thumb in her mouth again, and Lauren was crying.

29

"What's happening, Matt?" she asked as tears dripped down her cheeks.

Abbie pulled her thumb out of her mouth long enough to say, "I don't like it."

"Mom's upset because we went over the limit, isn't she?" asked Lauren. "Can Dad fix it?"

"I don't know," I said. "I hope so."

"I'm scared," said Lauren. "At school the other day— when we heard about that Lakeview girl who got taken— some kids were talking about families who go over their limit. They have to do all sorts of terrible things like sell their clothes and move out of their houses. And then the moms and dads have to go to jail."

"No one's taking Mom and Dad to jail," I said. At least I didn't think so. I'd never heard of people going to jail because of the limit.

"What's going to happen to us?" asked Lauren.

What could I possibly say—without lying—that would make it sound as if it wasn't a big deal? *No sweat. Our family's just about to fall apart. Don't worry.* Nope. Didn't quite cut it. It was like trying to explain away the danger of an F5 tornado barreling down on your house. Since scaring the girls wasn't my goal, I kept my mouth shut.

Lauren pouted her lips. "I hate the limit."

Mom walked very slowly out of the building and slumped into the car. "Karlene's the only one in the office. She said he's at the country club." Mom stared out the front window, three fingers pressed against her trembling lips. "I just don't know what to do."

She looked at me, as if I might have the answer. It was backward. Parents are supposed to know how to fix things, not kids.

"Let's go find Dad," I said.

A hint of a smile lifted one corner of her mouth. "That's a good idea. You've always been such a smart boy." She leaned over and pulled me to her with an arm around the back of my neck. "I love you, Matt."

"I . . . love you too." Her shoulder muffled my words. Why, exactly, were we saying this right now? I tried to pull away, but she clutched me tighter and held on for what seemed like a really long time.

Eventually we made it to the country club, Mom driving calmly and not breaking any traffic laws. We searched the parking lot but couldn't find Dad's car.

"We missed him." Mom pressed harder on the gas. "I bet he's back at the office by now."

During the next hour we drove back and forth between the country club and Dad's office, stopping to check out a restaurant Dad might have taken a client to whenever we saw one. Karlene stopped answering our phone calls, and I was surprised we didn't fill Dad's cell phone voice mail.

31

"Where is he?" Mom kept asking.

"Let's just go home," I said. "Maybe he's there."

"It's too early," she said. She glanced over her shoulder to make sure the girls weren't paying attention. Abbie had fallen asleep, and Lauren was deep into texting. "I'm afraid to go home without him."

"Let's go back to his office and wait," I said. "We can't keep driving around. You've probably used up a week's worth of our gas allotment already."

Mom's phone rang. She tried to grab it out of my hand, but I switched it to my far ear as I clicked it on.

"Hello?"

"Hey, Matt. What's up?"

"Dad!"

"William!" Mom let out such a big sigh of relief she could have filled a hot air balloon. I put the cell on speakerphone and held it up so Mom and Dad could talk.

"You guys seem a bit overeager to get in touch with me today. So what's the big news?" Dad's joking manner instantly put everyone at ease.

Except for Mom. She started crying. "We went over the limit at the store today. How could this happen, William? Didn't you say you were getting a deposit this morning from one of your clients?"

Dad's voice went ice cold. "Yes. I'll have Karlene find out what the glitch was. This has to be a mistake."

"I need you to come home right now," said Mom.

"Why?" he asked.

"Did you get a message from anyone besides us this afternoon?" she asked.

"Just a minute." We heard electronic beeps as Dad scanned his messages. "Yes. Here's one."

"Put us on hold and listen to it."

All went silent in the car. When Dad came back, his voice was as somber as when he spoke at my grandfather's funeral two years ago. "I'll get there as fast as I can."

"We're fifteen minutes from home," said Mom. "Are you at the office?"

"Yes. I'm leaving now. I'll be five minutes behind you."

For the first bit of the drive I asked Mom a bunch of questions—Lauren broke away from her phone long enough to ask a few too—but Mom never answered. She just shook her head and said she couldn't talk. Eventually we gave up. We drove the rest of the way in silence.

"Oh, my," said Mom as we turned the corner onto our street. "I didn't think they'd arrive so quickly. I thought we'd have time to call someone . . . to do something."

"Who?" I asked. Before I finished saying the word, I noticed the shiny black limo sitting in front of our house. The windows—even the front ones—were tinted too dark to see inside. "Do you know who it is?" I made

33

my voice sound stronger than I felt. Mom didn't answer. Slowing the car, she pulled into our driveway.

Abbie, awake again, bounced around like a rubber ball in the backseat. "Who is it, Mommy?"

Lauren sat rigid in her seat. Her arms made a tight X across her chest, and her eyebrows made a V in the middle of her forehead.

Mom didn't pull into the garage but stopped in the driveway underneath the basketball hoop.

She gave my thigh a tense squeeze. "Whatever happens, remember I love you. We're going to fix it."

"What's going to happen?" I asked, fumbling to unbuckle my seat belt.

She shot a glance at the limo, rubbing her lips together so hard her lipstick smudged. Heaving a deep sigh, she sagged against the headrest and closed her eyes. "I wish your father were here." After a few seconds she cleared her throat and sat up straight, tapping her closed fists against the steering wheel. "Okay," she said, more to herself than to us. She opened her door. "Listen, guys, I'm going to go talk to the people in the limousine. Stay in the car. Do you understand?"

"Why?" Abbie asked.

"Just do what she says," said Lauren.

Mom climbed out and shut the car door behind her. She took two steps away, came back, reopened the door, and pushed the lock button before closing it again.

I twisted a loose thread from the hem of my T-shirt around my finger as I watched Mom walk to the limo. She bent at the waist and talked to someone who sat in the front passenger's seat. Mom became very animated, throwing out her arms, shaking her head, looking up every few seconds for any sign of Dad's car.

Mom backed away as the limo door opened and a lady got out. No, it was more like she flowed out, because she moved in such a smooth, liquid way.

Honey, I thought, watching her slow, gliding motions. Her tan skin was only a few shades lighter than the light brown color of her suit. Her long, golden-brown hair rippled around her shoulders, like honey when you pour it and it mounds up on itself before settling flat.

I stared at her, my mouth hanging open. She looked like those ladies on TV and in magazines who try to sell us soft drinks, shoes, or dishwashers.

Honey Lady turned, her gaze hitting me like an unexpected pass in a basketball game, bam, right in the face. She walked toward me with even, flowing strides, Mom right beside her and talking all the while.

Honey Lady rapped lightly on the window. I looked at Mom, questioning. She dipped her chin in a small nod.

"You guys stay in here. Got it?" I said to the girls as I unlocked the car and climbed out.

"Are you Matthew?" Honey Lady asked with the warmest smile I've ever seen.

The breath in my nose sucked in fast and got stuck in my throat at the sound of her speaking my name. Her voice was thick and sweet and matched the rest of her just right. For a moment I wished I were fifteen years older and tall and covered with muscles.

I nodded.

"Hello. My name is Sharlene Smoot." She held out her hand to me, but I couldn't move. She lowered her arm. When she spoke again, her voice still came out smoothly, but it also contained authority. "Matthew, you are the oldest child of William and Rebecca Dunston, correct?"

"He is," said Mom. "But if you'll just wait a few minutes, my husband will be home. He'll explain the mix-up with our account. In fact, he probably has it fixed by now, if you'll just check."

Ignoring her, Honey Lady continued to direct her words toward me. "In light of the fact that your family unit has exceeded its debt limit and that option D of Federal Debt Ordinance 169 has been chosen for your rehabilitation, I must verify your identity and age."

"Can we at least discuss that option?" Mom asked, her voice growing frantic. "We'll happily go on supervised spending. I don't see why we're not allowed to choose our own rehabilitation option. I'd like to see some sort of legal explanation for why the choice was made for our family. What's so special about our circumstances?"

With a slow, fluid movement Honey Lady turned to look at Mom. "I'm sorry, I know this must be very upsetting for you, but I don't have that information. It's the responsibility of a different department. If you'd like, I'd be happy to e-mail you the contact information once I return to my office. I'm sure someone in that department will be able to answer all your questions. Now, Matthew, if you will please hold still." She smiled so sweetly I allowed her to take an eye scan as well as a handprint scan with a handheld unit. "Thirteen years old, correct?"

"Uh . . . yeah."

"Very good." She tapped a couple of things on her scanner. "All done."

That was it?

"I'll just go inside, then," I said.

Honey Lady held out her arm, blocking me against the car. I could have pushed past her, but I noticed a big man with gorilla muscles walking from the limo toward us. His small, dark eyes stared me into submission.

"What do you want me to do?" I asked.

"You are required to meet the obligations of FDO 169-D," said Honey Lady.

Thanks. That explains a whole lot.

"Once you understand all that entails, I think you will enjoy it," said Honey Lady. "I work for the FDRA. Our facility is very comfortable. It's practically brand-new and located only a couple of hours from here."

Well, hip-hip hooray for you.

"We'll be leaving now," Honey Lady said to Mom.

"Wait. Please. My husband will be here any second."

"There is nothing he can do or say that will change anything," said Honey Lady. "I'm sorry, but I do have a schedule. Come along, Matthew."

Come along? Was she nuts? Mom made a sound that was half scream, half sob. The girls, who still sat in the backseat of the car watching us through the window, started howling. I didn't care how pretty Honey Lady looked or how nice she sounded, I wasn't going anywhere with her. Even Gorilla Man couldn't force me.

I pushed through Honey Lady's outstretched arm like a grade-school kid playing Red Rover and sprinted toward the house. The next thing I knew, a couple of gorilla hands took hold of my shirt and held my shoulders in place, even though my legs fought for a few more steps. I kicked and punched and almost twisted out of my shirt, but Gorilla Man grabbed me tight around the chest, pinning my arms to my sides, and lifted me into the air.

In the background I heard Lauren and Abbie crying louder. They must have gotten out of the car. I'd told them to stay in there. Why hadn't they listened? Mom's voice became hysterical.

"Put him down. You're going to hurt him!"

"Resistance is to be expected," the honey voice said. "Don't worry. We're very experienced at dealing with it in a safe manner."

Gorilla Man dragged me to the open back door of the limo. With one of his massive arms he kept my upper body immobile; with the other he pressed down on my head, like cops do to criminals. A final shove sent me into the car. I landed, spread-eagled, halfway on the seat and halfway on the floor. Before I could twist around and sit up, he slammed the door behind me. The thump of the doors locking exploded in my ears. I lunged for the door, but it wouldn't open.

Lauren and Abbie screamed louder than ever; I could tell even though the car muffled the sound. Mom had fallen to her knees on the lawn. Honey Lady and Gorilla Man opened the doors to the front seats. I pounded on the window buttons, but they must have been disabled.

Dad's car pulled into the driveway, and I could breathe again. He'd gotten here on time. He could fix everything. His car had barely come to a stop when he jumped out and ran to Mom. She half stood, pointing at the limo. Dad sprinted over. Good. He'd talk some sense into Honey Lady. He'd make her let me go.

I stared at Dad, my hands plastered against the window. He couldn't see me, since the glass was so dark. He was close enough I could see a small twig snagged in his sweater-vest near his shoulder. I almost laughed. He must have spent some time in the brush at the golf course today. I sat back on the soft leather seat. This was almost over. My dad would save me.

He reached the sidewalk, almost close enough to touch me if the window had been down. The car moved beneath me.

Wait a minute!

I screamed out, "Dad!"

"Matt!" I could barely hear his voice. I tried the door handle again as I felt the limo drive away.

DAD RAN AFTER THE LIMO FOR A
block but couldn't keep up.

Lunging forward onto my knees, I
slammed my fist against the dark privacy
glass that separated the front seat from the back. "Stop!
Let me out of here!"

"For your safety, Matthew, I'd appreciate it if you
sat down and fastened your seat belt." The honey
voice flowed into the back part of the car through a
speaker.

*I don't care what you'd appreciate, so shut up and leave
me alone.* I picked up the heavy end of a seat belt and
chucked it. The strap kept it from doing any damage.
That didn't stop me from throwing it against the seat
again and again, grunting with my efforts.

"Matthew, please remain calm." Honey Lady's
voice was too sweet—like biting into a cube of pure
sugar. It made my teeth ache. "You can't hurt anything
in this vehicle. You can't hurt yourself." The voice took
on a shot of sour. "The only thing you can hurt by not

cooperating is your family. Now please sit down and fasten your seat belt."

They'd hurt Lauren and Abbie?

I let the seat belt drop. Still kneeling, I leaned the side of my head against the seat.

Honey Lady's voice, soft and smooth again, spoke to me. "You're doing a wonderful thing for your family, Matthew. You probably don't realize it, but you're saving them from financial devastation."

A tear sneaked out of the corner of my eye, slid over the bridge of my nose, and plopped onto the leather seat. I sniffed.

"Would you like a tissue?" asked Honey Lady.

"No," I said, sniffing more quietly. "I'm fine."

I heard a soft click. Honey Lady must've turned off the speaker. My upper body slid an inch to the right on the slick leather as the car turned and slowed down. The turn didn't feel sharp. It felt like the car had pulled over to the side of the road. The car stopped.

I heard the *ka-chunk ka-chunk* of one of the front doors being opened and closed. Then another *ka-chunk* as the door near me opened. Honey Lady crouched down and leaned inside, her face inches from where mine lay sideways on the seat. A few of her long, golden hairs tickled my nose. I turned my head the other way.

"Is it all right if I ride back here with you, now that you've settled down?" she asked.

"I don't care," I said. "It's not like I can stop you." Not when she had Gorilla Man backing her up. I scrambled to the other side of the limo and slumped against the window, my forehead resting on the cool glass.

I didn't watch, but I sensed her as she slid next to me, smooth as honey. I heard a click as she fastened her seat belt. A nice, flowery scent filled the space. She even smelled sweet. My fingers tightened into a fist. I wanted to punch something—maybe her or this limo or the limit. Anything.

A tap of Honey Lady's knuckles on the privacy glass signaled Gorilla Man to go. She turned toward me while stretching out her legs in the massive space in front of our seat. Okay, I peeked.

"I want you to understand the law and what's happening to you," she said, patting me on the arm and smiling a warm, sweet smile. "I want you to feel comfortable with me and your situation."

She kept her hand on my arm. It felt . . . good. I didn't know what to think. She acted nice—like she cared about me. She couldn't really, though, or she wouldn't have taken me away. And she wasn't just taking me from my family, she was also taking me from my friends, my school, my home—my life.

"Do you have any questions for me?" she asked.

Slumping, I jerked away from her touch and folded my arms across my chest. "Yeah. When can I go home?"

"That's the beauty of FDO 169-D!" Her smile would have lit up the bottom of a black pit. I almost wanted to squint away from it. "The amount of time you will be required to spend at the workhouse is entirely up to you and your family. The harder all of you work to get back under your debt limit, the sooner you can go home. I'm sure it makes you feel better to know you're in complete control of the situation. Doesn't it, Matthew?"

"Matt," I said, without really thinking.

"You like to be called Matt?"

"Yeah, I guess." I stiffened. "Whatever. So you're taking me to some workhouse?" History book pictures from the early 1900s of old factories appeared in my mind. The child laborers—child slaves really—always looked half starved and exhausted.

"Yes. FDO—Federal Debt Ordinance—169, option D, allows children of a certain age to help reduce their family's debt by spending some time at an FDRA work-house."

"What happened to options A through C? I thought families were supposed to be able to choose. I've heard stories, but I know of only one person for sure—a girl from Lakeview Middle School—who's had to go to a workhouse. Most families choose supervised spending. Why didn't *my* family get to choose?"

"Oh, Matt," she laughed and patted my arm again. "I know you overheard me tell your mother that I don't know why this option was chosen for your family." She leaned in close, twitching her eyebrows, and whispered, "Trust me. You'll like option D. FDRA workhouses are fabulous places to live—especially for kids like you." Her last word came out with a puff of air that tickled my ear. I leaned back until my head bumped against the glass.

"Wha . . . what's FDRA?"

"It stands for Federal Debt Rehabilitation Agency. It's where I work. We oversee those participating under FDO 169-D."

She went on and on about how amazing this workhouse was and how much I was going to love it there. After a few minutes I tuned her out. One thing I knew for sure, no place could be as much of a paradise as she seemed to think the workhouse was. I stared out the window. Soon we were speeding down the freeway, heading for the city. Honey Lady pulled out a case she'd brought with her from the front seat. It contained a portable movie player for me and a laptop for her. I only half watched the movie as my mind planned my next move. They were dead wrong if they thought I'd skip along happily to some slave-labor camp. No way, suckers. Just like Nana, I wasn't about to go without a fight.

My movie was nearing the end when Gorilla Man pulled the limo onto an exit ramp. He had to stop at a light at the end of the ramp. That's when I made my move, yanking on the door handle with all my might. My muscles burned with the effort, and I slammed my shoulder into the door—again and again. It didn't budge. I'd thought that when Honey Lady climbed in back with me, maybe she'd left the doors unlocked. She hadn't. It didn't matter. I kept slamming.

"Matt." Honey Lady slid her arms around me, coaxing me away from the door. How could arms be so strong and so soft at the same time? She drew me in close, like a mother comforting her upset child. She whispered soft sounds into my hair and rocked me for just a second, enough for me to unclench my fingers and let go of the door handle. "You're going to be okay." The mother in her disappeared and the sales-pitch woman returned. "I'm so excited for you. We're almost to the workhouse. Just wait until you see it. You're very lucky, you know. Six months ago you would have had to take an airplane to a workhouse in the east. Now they're building them all over the place. Some people still have to travel much farther than you've had to—since our workhouse serves the entire Midwest area."

I wriggled out of her grasp and turned back to the window, calculating the average number of windows for the buildings we passed. It wasn't hard, since we had to drive slowly because of the traffic, and the buildings we drove by were small—eight floors, max. The really big skyscrapers stood clustered together in the distance. A few flower beds and trees appeared every once in a while between the buildings. I even saw a small park. Green and space nudged out steel and cement more and more as we drove.

"There it is," said Honey Lady.

Even though I tried to keep my eyes sulkily staring at the piece of lint on the floor by my shoe, I couldn't stop myself from glancing out the window on Honey Lady's side of the car, following her gaze. At least I could *sound* unimpressed.

"Yeah, it's a building. So what?" I fought for every ounce of boredom I could squeeze into my voice. This was no child slave-labor workhouse. The silver and glass building sat almost glowing in the growing darkness. A wide spread of grass stretched out around it, and trees grew everywhere. Lampposts lit up the grounds like a ballpark. A clump of trees stood in the middle of the front lawn. Short trees straddled the walkway to the building from the parking lot. A whole bunch of trees—enough to make a small forest—stretched up tall and strong behind it.

"Home, sweet home," said Honey Lady as Gorilla Man pulled off the street.

Home? Not for me. Never. Even if I had to spend the rest of my life here, this building would never be home.

A security arm blocked our entrance into the parking lot. Through the side window I watched as Gorilla Man's hand reached out and his long fingers punched a few keys on a keypad that hung from the end of a white, candy-cane-shaped pole. A narrow red laser beamed out to scan his retina. The gate lifted.

With only three other cars parked in the small lot, Gorilla Man pulled lengthwise across the spaces closest to the curving cement walk that led to the building entrance.

Honey Lady let out a little-girl squeal and gave my knee a sharp squeeze. "We're here!" She sprang out of the car, seeming to have forgotten about her laptop. Maybe Gorilla Man would clean up after her. I followed, leaving the portable movie player behind as well. I didn't have a suitcase to fetch from the trunk, so we headed straight up the walkway.

A few feet in front of the wide glass doors Honey Lady pulled a remote out of her pocket and pushed some buttons. She froze for a second while a laser scanned her eye. The doors slid open.

"Come on in, Matt," she said, gesturing with her hand like a butler on TV.

Okay. I had to admit, nice place. It reminded me of the lobby of the five-star hotel we'd gone to for Aunt Rachael's wedding last summer—every surface sparkly or plush or polished.

"One minute," Honey Lady said. Her heels clicked across the marble floor as she crossed the wide room to what would have been the reception desk at a hotel.

I sauntered through a grouping of furniture—sofas, chairs, end tables. The marble tops of the tables reminded me of the big marble slab Nana pulls out around Christmastime to make candy—the marble keeps the candy's heat down. I ran my hand over the smooth top. Not as cool as I expected. My fingers slipped around the edge of the table.

Ouch!

I jerked my hand up to my face, holding it with the other hand. A bee sting? In here? I looked closer. A thin, brown sliver had imbedded itself in the pad of my index finger. Since when did marble have slivers? Fake piece of junk. Honey Lady was still occupied with the scowling, grumpy lady behind the reception desk—what a crab—so after I pulled out the sliver, I wandered through the rest of the lobby, discovering that all the plants were synthetic, the bright candy in a dish was glass, and the Zen water feature was a holograph.

Yeah, nice place.

"Okay, Matt, let's get you settled." Honey Lady's rah-rah cheerleader voice drowned out the clicking of her heels as she scurried away from the desk. With that butler arm she guided me to a hallway off the right side of the lobby. The thing went on forever, like a tunnel into nowhere.

I backed up a step. Crab Woman, behind the reception desk, barked something into some sort of speaker as she sprang to her feet, making the reading glasses that dangled from a chain around her neck sway back and forth. She seemed older than mom age, but younger than grandmother age. A second later Gorilla Man lumbered into the room and stood, staring me down, with his overmuscled arms folded high across his chest.

"Come on, Matt." Honey Lady wrapped one arm around my shoulder and leaned in close to my ear, speaking in that airy voice of hers that made me want to pull away. "I know you're going to love it here. We're so glad you've joined us. Why don't you take a look at your room and give this place a chance before you decide you hate it? Hmm?"

I shrugged my answer, mostly to nudge her arm off.

"Good choice. Come on!" *Rah, rah.* With a flick of

one hand she waved Gorilla Man back to whatever hole he'd crawled out of. I filed that bit of info away for later as we started down the hall—Gorilla Man wasn't permanently camped out in the lobby. Maybe it emptied out completely at times—like late at night.

Honey Lady led me past one door before she stopped and opened another one. I stretched around her to get a look inside. Not bad. Not amazing, but not bad. Besides a bed, the room held one large bookshelf full of books and another one of video games. The TV wasn't nearly as big as the one in the family room back home, but almost as big as the one Mom and Dad had in their bedroom. A computer sat on a small table next to the head of the bed.

"This is where you'll spend the first night—tonight." Honey Lady walked across the room and opened a door near the far corner. "Here's your private bathroom." She walked around the end of the bed to the computer table. "Use this remote to access TV programs or movies. And here"—she turned on the computer and sat down—"I'll show you how to order dinner. You'll also need to order clothes and toiletries—anything you think you might need before tomorrow. In the morning you'll take your test and get your permanent assignment."

Test? Permanent assignment? Great. Something else to worry about. *I hope your floors are thick, Honey*

Lady, or else my pacing tonight will wear a hole right through them.

"Don't be shy, Matt, come on in here." She'd pulled up the Midwest FDRA workhouse's home page by the time I shuffled to the desk. I ran my fingers over the top of the monitor. Sweet machine, especially for a temp room. The process for ordering food from nearby restaurants and clothes and toiletries from nearby stores was so easy I focused more on checking out the computer than listening to Honey Lady's explanation—until the end.

"Of course, the laser will scan your eye after you order."

"Oh, uh, I think my parental permission card is almost empty." I'd used it to buy lunch at school today— was it really only today?—and the lunch lady had warned me that I was running close to empty.

"You don't need a parental permission card here," said Honey Lady.

No way. Kids always had to present a card, or slide one into a computer slot, before they could get an eye scan to buy anything. Otherwise, what was to stop us from going out and buying a new game room full of gadgets every time we felt like it?

She stood up. "Don't forget pajamas and underwear when you're ordering your clothes." She winked at me and pulled out the chair for me to sit down. "Would you like me to wait here with you until your dinner arrives?"

"No. I'll just surf the Web or watch TV."

"All right, then. I'll be in my office for another hour or so. If you need anything, pick up that phone by the bed and ask to be connected to me. Do you remember my name?"

"Yes." No, wait. They'd think I was nuts if I asked for Honey Lady. "I guess not."

"Sharlene Smoot," she said as she ruffled the hair on the top of my head. I twitched away to let her know I didn't like it. The hands lifted from my head and settled on my shoulders.

I shrugged them off of there, too. "You can leave now." I fixed my eyes on the monitor as my fingers started going at the keyboard.

"All right. If that's what you want. Listen, go to bed soon after dinner, and make sure you get a good night's sleep. The testing will last all day tomorrow, and it's important for you to do your best. Good night. And Matt, I can tell you're going to love being a member of our FDRA family."

CHAPTER 06

THE MEAT LOAF I'D ORDERED FOR dinner didn't taste right. Mom made a killer meat loaf. It's what I asked for anytime she gave me a choice.

The gravy-drenched bite of meat turned to glue in my mouth as I pictured eating at home with my family. Dinnertime had come and gone ages ago, but everyone in my family had probably been too upset to eat anything. At least they'd better have lost their appetites. Abbie should be in bed by now. I bet she'd been too scared to sleep alone in her room. Lauren would let her sleep with her. What were Mom and Dad doing? Making phone calls, doing Internet searches, and examining every single cent in their account, I hoped.

I shoved the plate of food away and jumped to my feet. Why weren't there any windows in this room? The other floors had windows. I'd seen the light glowing through them from the outside.

I paced a nervous circle around the room, like a rat

in a cage, trapped and cut off from the world I knew, not knowing what the people in control had in store for me.

Wait a minute, I thought as I dug my cell phone out of my front pocket. I wasn't completely cut off. I don't know why I hadn't thought of my phone earlier. I stared at the buttons for a few seconds, deciding who to call first. Two questions burned in my brain. One, what was my family doing? And two, what was everyone at school saying about me—would I ever be able to show my face there again?

Duh, idiot. Although I felt as if a week had gone by since Honey Lady showed up at my house, only hours, not days, had passed. No one at school was saying anything about me, because no one had been to school since I'd been taken. I'd wait and call Brennan or Lester tomorrow.

I pulled up my home phone number and anxiously waited to hear a familiar voice. Instead I heard nothing. I looked at my screen. *No signal.* Oh, come on. Wait a minute. A landline phone sat right by the bed. I picked it up and punched a few buttons.

Crab Woman's voice came on, making me wince. "You need something?"

"I was . . . just trying to call someone," I said.

"This is an in-house line only." She hung up, the loud *click* making my eardrum ring.

Sweet dreams to you, too, Crab Woman.

Well, I knew the computer worked at least. If Abbie hadn't forced Lauren to come to bed when she did, chances were good that Lauren was online. I sent her a message, just asking if she was there.

Ten seconds went by. Then twenty. *Come on, Lauren. Be online.* Shoot. Maybe Brennan was online. A knock at my door pulled me away from the computer. It ended up being a delivery person who handed over several wrapped paper packages in shiny blue-and-white-striped shopping bags. The new clothes I'd ordered—pajamas for tonight and jeans and a T-shirt for tomorrow. Socks and boxers too. And a toothbrush and toothpaste.

After I closed the door and tossed the packages onto my bed, I walked back to the door. I opened it again— just a couple of inches. And closed it. Huh. I opened it and closed it again.

My mind started calculating. Distance equals rate times time—one of the most basic math formulas in the world. *The distance between this door and the end of the hallway—about fifteen feet. Plus another fifty feet to get to the front sliding glass doors equals sixty-five feet.* I could do an eight-second fifty-yard dash. Converting to feet made a rate of 18.75 feet per second. Dividing the distance by the rate gave me a time of 3.47 seconds. I figured I should round up to five or six seconds to allow for the fact that I'd have to turn a corner and dodge a chair or two. Would that be fast enough to make it outside before Crab Woman caught up with me? If she wore high heels like Honey Lady, I'd make it out no problem. Now, Gorilla Man—if he happened to be in the lobby, I'd be toast.

I slid into the chair in front of the computer and cracked my knuckles. Time to do one of the things I did best: in-depth online snooping—okay, call it hacking, if you must. I just needed to break into this workhouse's files, and I was sure to find some sort of Gorilla Man guard-duty schedule that would let me know if I was home free or shut down.

It took longer than I'd anticipated to get in, but I found it—not the minute-by-minute breakdown of Gorilla Man's location I was hoping for, but a schedule that listed guard A's assigned duty in the monitoring room for this evening along with guard B's duties today in backup monitoring and retrieval. "Retrieval," a polite way to say "kidnapping." So guard B would be Gorilla Man. If I understood this schedule correctly, both guards should be safely stashed away in a monitoring room right now. *Well, workhouse, it's been real, but the time has come for me to make my exit.*

I slipped into the hall and eased the door silently closed behind me. Instead of breaking into a sprint right away, I realized a better idea would be to sneak down this hall and then make a break for it once I emerged into the lobby. That would cut the response time Crab Woman had to chase me down or call for a guard.

Hugging the wall, I crept nearly noiselessly toward the wide arching opening at the end of the hall that led to the lobby. I paused in the shadows out of reach of the lobby light, near the opening. Holding my breath, I listened. I couldn't hear anything other than Crab Woman barking some instructions to someone over her intercom system. Good. If she was distracted, that gave me just that much more of an edge. Stepping forward, I took a quick peek. No Gorilla Man in sight.

A nagging thought nudged at one corner of my brain. Where, exactly, did I think I was going to go once I burst through those glass doors? What harm was going to happen to my family if I didn't stay here? I shoved those thoughts aside. I'd make it home somehow. Mom and Dad would want me there. They'd take care of the rest of the mess.

Another step, another look around. Crab Woman had stopped talking, but she'd shifted her attention to her computer. No one else in sight. This was it. The best chance I was going to get. I took another second to pump myself up. *Go. Go now!* My leg muscles tensed, ready to spring.

The heavy thumps of big feet moving fast threw me back into my shadowy hiding spot like a punch in the chest. I froze, not even breathing—waiting for those gorilla hands to reach around the corner and grab me. The blood pounding in my ears obscured the sound of the footsteps. It took me a second to realize they'd disappeared, replaced by the sound of clicking high heels across the tile.

"What's the big emergency now?" Crab Woman's gravelly voice asked.

"A Third Floor." It was Honey Lady. "Fourteen-year-old boy. Seizure."

"Another one? It was easier when they just got headaches. You going to have to dump this one too?"

"I'm not sure yet. We'll bring him down to a holding room tonight and keep a close watch on him. If worse comes to worst, we'll have to demote him to the first floor."

"Too bad."

I didn't hear anything else—no more talking. No Honey Lady heels walking away. Guess she wasn't going anywhere for a while. I'd have to wait until later and try again. Maybe in the middle of the night—that probably would have been the smarter move to begin with. Sliding my feet, I inched backward to my room. When I felt the door handle behind me I eased it open. Whoops.

59

Wrong room. This one was small, with only a desk and a computer. The door closed with a clunk that brought my shoulders to my ears. The sound seemed to echo through the long, empty hallway forever.

Crab Woman appeared in the opening to the lobby so fast she nearly scared the eyebrows off my face. I yanked my hand away from the incorrect door handle and thrust it behind my back, as if I held something I needed to hide. She stood with her hands on her hips and her elbows sticking out at her sides.

Her voice came out harsh and cold. "Going somewhere?"

I shook my head.

"Then get back in your room!" She threw out an arm to point me to the correct door. She didn't have to tell me twice. My feet couldn't get me behind my closed bedroom door fast enough.

So much for trying to make another escape later. Now they'd be watching me too closely. *Idiot! Way to blow your perfect chance.*

Half an hour later I heard a scuffling in the hall. It slowly made its way past my room. Pausing my video game I slid my door open an inch, just enough to get a glimpse into the hall.

Gorilla Man led a teenager down the hall to the

room just past mine. The kid was groaning. Both his hands were pressing tightly against the sides of his head. Honey Lady followed close behind them.

"You're going to be fine now, Tyson. The medication we gave you should be kicking in soon. A good night's sleep is all you need." I could just imagine that overly enthusiastic cheerleader smile of hers, even though all I could see was the back of her head. *Go, team!* As soon as Gorilla Man took the kid inside the room, Honey Lady turned on her heel and walked away. My door had eased open to a couple of inches, and I jerked it back to a crack. I still could see Honey Lady's face as she briskly walked by. Her frown was deep, and her lips were pinched tightly. She looked like she wanted to punch someone. I slid my door silently shut. I sure as heck didn't want it to be me.

CHAPTER 07

YOUR TEST IS NOW COMPLETE.

I sat back in the chair, stretching my arms out on either side of me, my eyes remaining on the bright red words flashing across the middle of the screen. Finally, after hours stuck in this bland little room with nothing but a computer, I'd finished. It hadn't been as bad as I'd expected.

When Honey Lady had led me into this room right after breakfast, she'd explained that the test became increasingly difficult as it progressed and that I'd eventually come up against some tasks that I wouldn't be able to complete. Yeah, a test that's designed to make you fail. What kid doesn't dream about that? In his nightmares, maybe.

I did get stuck a couple of times, but not until late in the afternoon. Any task that required me to do something artsy or creative—like graphic design or computer animation—had me stymied. It was never long before Honey Lady—or whoever it was monitoring my work through a computer link in another room—would send me a message saying they were moving me on to my next task—something logical, like programming, or manipulating software so I could compute a super-hard math problem, which I'd zip right through.

My fingers tapped the armrests of my chair. *So what happens now? How long before Honey Lady comes in and tells me the results—and just what exactly will those results mean?* Part of me wished for more problems to appear on the screen. Those I could deal with. How well I did on this test had been totally up to me. I had no say in our family money issues. I hadn't been able to prevent Gorilla Man from shoving me into the back of the limo.

I spun my chair around to face the door. What was keeping Honey Lady? I spun around in a complete circle. The door remained closed. Was that sick kid locked behind some other closed door in this hallway? Last night, when I went into my bathroom, I could hear him moaning through the wall. It made me wonder if he should go to the hospital, but I never heard anyone come and get him during the night. I hope that meant he got better. They *would* take us to the doctor if we got sick, wouldn't they? I mean, that would be child abuse if they didn't. *Right.* Like what's in the kid's best interest matters to anyone in the government.

The door burst open. "Matt, you did great!" Honey Lady click-clicked across the floor on her high heels and threw her arms around me. "I knew you could do it. You made top floor!"

I almost felt obligated to jump to my feet, clap my hands, and cheer along with her. *Go, fight, win!*

I stayed firmly planted in my chair. "What exactly does that mean?"

"I'm sorry," she said with a giggle that reminded me of Lauren when she's on the phone with her girlfriends. "Of course you don't understand what I'm talking about. I'm just so excited for you. Top Floors are few and far between. You're going to love it on the top floor. It's where the brightest, most gifted children live and work. You get to do the most rewarding tasks. The work is the most difficult, by far, but all our Top Floors enjoy the challenge. That's the kind of kids they are—it's the kind of kid *you* are. That's why we group you together. We find you tend to get along best with peers on your own intellectual level."

"Like . . . what kind of work do we have to do?" The schoolbook child slave-laborers, pushing heavy wagons full of yarn around giant, noisy machines, popped into my mind again.

"Come on," she said, with a wave of her hand. "I'll explain more while we walk. I can't wait to get you up there."

She pulled me from my chair and led me out of the

room. Her grip around my wrist seemed tight enough to cut the circulation to my hand. I wiggled my fingers, just to make sure I still could.

Bright sunshine from big windows covering the front of the building reflected off all the silver surfaces in the lobby, making the entire room sparkle and shine. If a room could look happy, this one did. In fact, it looked too happy, like it was trying too hard. The wide front doors and the world outside them attracted my eyes. *Later. Too many grown-ups around now.*

"We've got a new Top Floor here," Honey Lady called out, her voice all bouncy and bubbly. Crab Woman looked up, not even trying to hide the sour look on her face.

"Good for you," she said in that sharp, sarcastic tone of hers.

Honey Lady flipped her long, flowing hair and, ignoring her, guided me across the lobby to a short hallway.

"Emergency stairs are there." She pointed to a closed door. "Here's the elevator. You're already programmed into it."

Programmed into an elevator? That was new. Honey Lady pushed a button, and the doors slid open for us to step inside. The elevator had no floor buttons.

"Say your full name, loud and clear," she said.

"Matthew Dunston."

The elevator moved.

"Well done," she said. "You will now be taken directly to your floor. It works the same way if you ever need to go down—say your name and it will take you to the lobby. You'll rarely need to use it, though. You work, live, and spend your leisure time on the top floor—you really have no reason to leave it."

My feet moved back a few steps. This top floor place was starting to sound like a prison. "I can't leave the top floor?"

"I didn't say that," she said. "I said you have no *reason* to leave it. If in the future you develop a need to leave, just check with me. There is a certain protocol for these things. I'll help you make the arrangements and fill out the forms. But, as I said before, besides in an emergency, I really can't think of a reason for you to leave your floor."

"This sounds complicated. How many forms would I have to fill out if I wanted to go outside?"

Honey Lady laughed. "Oh, Matt. You're making a bigger deal of it than it is. We just need to keep track of our workhouse residents. Unless they get permission and complete the paperwork, each child needs to remain on their assigned floor. It's a safety issue."

It still sounded complicated to me. I couldn't just
pop downstairs and ride my bike whenever I felt like it.

Then again, I didn't have my bike with me. I didn't have anything of my own with me. No one I knew, either. It was like starting over in a brand-new life. My stomach bounced up and down along with the elevator. Was there a garbage can in here in case I needed to throw up?

Ding.

"Here we are," said Honey Lady as the elevator doors slid open.

Ugly, gray cement walls—without a single window—stretched in front of me as far as I could see. My prison cell. I shuffled away from the door until I bumped into the back of the elevator. Honey Lady had already disappeared into the hallway and around a gray corner. The only thing worse than walking into that dark top floor was being left here alone.

The instant the last part of my body cleared the elevator door, it swooshed closed behind me. It must've been weight or motion sensitive. If I hadn't been in such a panic I would've stopped to get a better look at the cool tech.

I sprinted around the corner into another dim hall. I didn't even look; I just ran. Two seconds later, bam, I found her.

"Oh, there you are," she said, smiling sweetly down at me. "Ready for the top floor?"

Without waiting for an answer, she pushed through

the heavy swinging metal door that stood at the end of the hall.

I had to squint. Nobody told me I'd need sunglasses up here. The room was so full of light I thought for a second we'd gone too far and ended up on the roof. My eyes adjusted quickly and allowed me to begin processing all the sights and sounds of the top floor. We stood in a huge room with a high ceiling covered with skylights. A double row of cubicles ran down the middle of it. The cubicles were covered with typical blue-gray fabric, except the closest one. It was completely enclosed and made out of glass panels. What's the point of having a cubicle made of glass if you're going to cover the walls with blinds? And close them all?

"Work is over for the day," said Honey Lady. "The other kids are eating or playing somewhere. Except . . ." She paused at the glass cube and knocked on the sliding door. "Reginald?" Honey Lady called. "You in there?"

A deep voice answered back. "Yes, ma'am."

"I thought so," said Honey Lady. Lowering her voice she said, "Reginald loves his computer. He loves his privacy, too. That's why he has the special setup. Respect his wishes and give him his space."

I followed her as she proceeded down the row of cubicles. They were big. I'd seen Brennan's dad's cubicle once, and it was probably half the size of one of these.

"Boys on this side, girls on the other." Honey Lady pointed briefly as she power-walked toward the other side of the top floor. She seemed to be in a big hurry all of a sudden. "Now, if I can just find some of our other Top Floors to drop you off with, we'll be all set." Pausing in front of a glass door with a metal bar across the middle, she turned to me, her all-business face morphing into the super-sweet, sugar-coated one. "I just know you're going to love this room." She reached a long-nailed finger out to poke me in the shoulder—attempting playfulness, I guess. "It's a favorite with our Top Floors."

As she pushed through the door—and pulled me after her—a soft wave of warm wet air wrapped around us. No way. A swimming pool? Inside a building? On the top floor? The pool had a diving board and a big slide that curved a couple of times on the way down. A raised hot tub sat in the far corner, spilling a waterfall into the pool. This was beyond amazing. The entire ceiling and the outside wall were pure windows. Even though the sun was starting to set, the room sparkled with light. There were even girls here, wearing bathing suits! Wait until I told the guys back home about this. They'd all beg their parents to go over their limits.

"Miss Smoot. Hi, Miss Smoot!" Three girls who looked close to my age climbed out of the pool and ran over to Honey Lady.

"Hello, girls," said Honey Lady. "This is Matt. He just made top floor today. Madeline, Paige, and Neela." She pointed to each girl. Madeline crinkled her nose—nothing different here than at my school, where the girls snubbed me. Paige smiled a little and waved, though. The last girl, Neela, nodded her head, like a queen to a loyal subject. In fact—wow—now that I looked at her, she was pretty enough to be royalty. With that rich golden-brown skin and all that dark hair she could be a princess from India. *Do they have princesses in India?*

"Hi," Madeline said in a flat tone before flipping her wet hair and turning to speak with much more enthusiasm to Honey Lady. "Do you like my new bathing suit, Miss Smoot?" She turned around, stopping and posing a couple of times like a model. "I just got it this morning."

"Very nice," said Honey Lady. "That color really complements your skin tone."

Raising her chin, the girl smiled smugly. "I chose the color after I did a beauty analysis on myself at the Cluminair Cosmetics website. Cluminair is a new company I found while doing my research assignment for the P and N Brokerage Company last week. I recommended it as an investment to consider. I hope they looked into it, because Cluminair's stock went up eight points in two days."

"P and N did take your advice. They're very pleased

with your work. So am I. Keep it up." Honey Lady's smile flattened out instantly as she turned to the Indian princess. "Neela, did you receive the message I sent you this morning?"

"Yes." The girl's voice was barely audible.

"And what do you plan to do to remedy the situation?"

"I'll finish the mock-up on the spread first thing tomorrow." She spoke in a one-hundred-percent American accent—there went my Indian princess theory.

"You'd better. You're two days late as it is."

"I will. I promise."

Honey Lady continued with the lecture, even though Neela had told her straight out that she'd take care of whatever problem it was she was having. *Blah, blah, blah. Get your work done on time. Be responsible. Blah, blah.* Adults were the same everywhere. How long was this going to take?

I pulled out my cell phone and tried to text Brennan. Still nothing. Weird in the middle of the city. That last girl—Paige, I think her name was—watched me mess with my phone. She crinkled her lips and shook her head.

"All right, then!" Paige and I both jumped at Honey Lady's rah-rah voice. "I've got to run, girls. You'll look after Matt, here, won't you? Show him around. Make him feel at home."

"What? Ew!" said Madeline. "We're in our bathing suits!"

Turning pink, Paige crossed her arms over herself.

"Besides, we're not done swimming yet. Can't you find one of the boys?" Madeline grabbed Paige by the arm and dragged her toward the pool. She leaned into Paige's ear but looked straight at me and spoke plenty loud. "Maybe if she brought us someone cute every once in a while. What is it with nerdy guys and the top floor?"

With that the two girls jumped into the pool. A second later, when their heads surfaced, Madeline called out, "Come on, Neela!"

Neela shook her head, rubbing her temple. "I'm going to sit in the hot tub for a while."

She kept rubbing the side of her head as she walked away. Honey Lady and I moved toward the door. Looked like Neela had a headache. I hoped it wasn't too bad. She was right, though. I bet a soak in the hot tub would help her feel better.

Headaches. Crab Woman's voice from the night before grated like gravel in my mind: *It was easier when they just got headaches. You going to have to dump this one too?*

Could something about this building be making kids sick?

CHAPTER 08

"DO YOU KNOW WHY MY CELL PHONE isn't working?" I asked Honey Lady as we pushed through the door and out of the pool room.

"We've always had trouble getting reception here," she said. "Never could figure out why. Feel free to use your computer if you need to communicate with someone outside the workhouse." The cool air of the cubicle room on my moist clothing sent a shiver through my body. "Let's see, where would they . . ." Her heels would have been clicking rapidly if we weren't walking on carpet. Another door stood within a couple of yards of the pool-room door. Honey Lady yanked this one open too. "Aha! I knew it."

Two boys were running around in the large gym. They held rackets and were taking turns hitting a ball attached to a long bungee cord that snapped the ball off in wild directions. I should say only one boy—the taller boy, with blond, shaggy hair—hit the ball. He hit it a lot. The other boy—much shorter, with straight dark hair and almond eyes behind thin glasses—ducked every time the ball came near him. He swung a couple of times but didn't connect.

"Boys! Stop and come over here," said Honey Lady. The short boy did, but the tall blond boy got in a few more whacks before he finally lowered his racket. Honey Lady pointed to him as he ran over. "This is Henry." The shorter boy shuffled up alongside him. "And this is Jeffery."

"Hey," said the tall boy, nodding his chin at me. He turned a wicked grin toward Honey Lady and rubbed his hands together. "You've finally brought us a new Top Floor to torture."

"Very amusing," said Honey Lady without cracking a smile. "This is Matt." She pushed me forward a few inches with her hand on my shoulder. "I need to get back downstairs. Please show him around and fill him in on how things work around here."

"Hey, wait—" Before I could remember Honey Lady's real name and call her back to make her answer the dozens of questions I couldn't even begin to put into words, she'd click-clicked right out the door. I turned to the guys.

The tall one held up his racket, moving it in small circles. "Jeffery, you go in on the left, and I'll attack from the right. Ready?"

What the heck? Ducking, I shuffled back a few quick

steps while lifting both arms to shield my head. Talk about bullies and cruel initiation rites.

Jeffery swung his racket up over his shoulder, holding it tight with both hands and advancing fast on me.

"Whoa, Jeffery, hold up, man." The tall guy, Henry, stretched out one arm to block him. "I was just messing with the new boy's brain." He gave me a soft punch to the shoulder. "No lie, dude, I'm glad you're here. Now I'm not the newest newbie on the floor. You'll be even more clueless than me." He gave his head a cocky little shake. "Make me look good."

Frowning, Jeffery reluctantly lowered his racket.

I gulped, trying to hide the fact that I was still breathing hard. "N-no problem." I stood up straighter and shook out my arms. "How long have you guys been here?"

"Going on two months," Henry said. "Jeffery's been here about twice that long. Don't worry. I've got the system down. I'll let you in on all the insider secrets."

"You're so clueless you don't even know if there *are* any secrets," Jeffery said.

Henry waved him off. "You play paddle-wall-ball?" he asked me. "Jeffery here doesn't put up much of a challenge. I've gotta find me a worthy opponent."

Jeffery pushed his glasses up his nose. "I'm getting better."

"I've never played." I'd seen paddle-wall-ball on TV.

It's a cross between racquetball and a giant paddleball. I think the courts cost a ton. There weren't a lot of them around. "Looks fun."

"Cool. Go change and we'll play."

"Change?"

"Your clothes, dude!"

I stared down at my jeans and T-shirt.

"He just got here," said Jeffery. "Obviously he's ignorant about the procedure to order clothes."

"No, I'm not. I just haven't had the time to do much of it yet." Hitching my thumb, I turned my head toward the door. "Should I go use one of those cubicle computers?"

"Whoa, man, you can't just use any computer out there. You've gotta stick with your own—it's sort of an unwritten rule, like sticking with your own toothbrush. Use your own cubie comp or use the one in your room."

"I have a computer in my room, too?" Cool.

"He doesn't know anything," said Jeffery.

Henry draped one arm around my shoulder and turned me to the door. "Let's go get you caught up on the way things roll here on the top floor. Maybe a little tour? You up to playing tour guide, Jeffery?"

"Go ahead," the short kid said, waving us off as he headed out the door. "Have fun with your new best buddy, Coop."

"Coop? I thought your name was Henry."

"Cooper. Henry Cooper. I don't like Henry. You eat yet, bro?"

"Dinner? No. And it's Matt."

He must have forgotten.

"Well, come on, bro. Let's go order us an extra-large with pepperoni and get you some gym clothes."

Long strings of chewy mozzarella stretched between my teeth and the piece of pizza in my hand. Lifting it high, I drizzled cheese into my mouth and chewed fast. Across the table Coop smiled through the long strands of mozzarella hanging off his chin.

"Maybe we shouldn't have ordered triple cheese," I said after managing to swallow.

"Naw, this is the only way to go." Coop gulped down a swig of soda on top of his food.

We'd had the pizza delivered to my bedroom.

My bedroom. What an understatement. It was practically an apartment—my own bachelor pad. If only I could invite the guys from school here for a few minutes to let them see how I was going to be living now. Talk about one-upping—this was more like ten-upping, or twenty-upping. Nobody was ever going to beat me. The only thing this place didn't have was a kitchen, but who needed one? Top Floors ordered all their meals over the computer, like I'd done downstairs.

Speaking of meals: "I think tomorrow I'll order some of the barbecue that guy in the glass cubicle had delivered to him. Sure smelled good. What's with that guy anyway? Why would you want to eat dinner in your cubicle? Unless he's got something amazing hidden behind those blinds."

"Nothing could be amazing enough to keep me boxed up all day long. This is as much as I can take." He knocked the side of his fist against the big window next to us at the table, which had a great view of the lush lawns and thick trees we'd never be able to run through without first filling out a pile of forms. "At least we have the paddle-wall-ball court." Coop stood and walked over to the remote control sitting on the arm of the leather sofa. He punched a button and changed the channel on the huge flat screen on my wall from a music video to a sports program. I'd have a clear view of the TV screen from my bed, too, if I ever decided to watch from there.

"That guy—what's his name?—he stays in his cubicle *all day*?"

"All day, every day," said Coop, going for another piece of pizza. "Miss Smoot calls him Reginald. The rest of us just call him nutcase."

"He has to come out sometime. To sleep? To go to the bathroom. He's *got* to go to the bathroom."

"Maybe he has a bladder the size of the swimming

pool." Coop picked a huge chunk of sausage off his slice and popped it into his mouth. "He does come out at night. He sleeps in his room. Does other things in there too, a little. Haven't figured out what yet."

"Why don't you just ask him?"

Coop sputtered out a laugh, spewing tiny flecks of half-chewed mozzarella and pepperoni. Good thing the table was big enough that none of it reached me.

"Ask him? Bro, nobody talks to Reginald. When he's working in that glass box of his, it's like . . . sacred. You can't disturb him unless the workhouse is on fire—and even then it's iffy. Once Isaac—who's in the cubie next to him—knocked on his glass door and tried to invite him to come play laser tag in the gym with him and Kia. Reginald didn't make a sound, and within a minute one of the security dudes was up here cutting Isaac down."

"Okay, then, no biggie. Just ask him when he comes out."

"Right." Dropping the remainder of his slice onto the table with a splat, Coop leaned forward on his elbows. "If you ever catch sight of him, let me know. I'll hustle over and give him an interview."

"No way. You're saying you've never seen him? In two whole months?"

"I'm saying."

"Surely someone . . ."

Slumping back in his chair, he shook his head, flipping out his shaggy blond hair.

"I'll be the first, then."

"Go for it, dude. Hey, how about going to my room and playing some vids while we wait for your gym clothes?" Coop scooped up the remainder of his cheese-smothered piece of pizza.

"Sure." I was always up for video games. Sitting back in my chair, I pulled out my cell again and fiddled with it. Nothing. "Do you *ever* get a signal here?"

"Haven't yet."

"Doesn't that seem really weird?"

"No. Isaac thinks there's a huge alien spaceship hovering over the workhouse that blocks the signal. I just think there's a glitch that could be fixed easy enough if Miss Smoot wanted it to get fixed. I'm guessing she thinks our work quota would go down if we could talk and text all we wanted."

"Huh," I said, sticking the phone back in my pocket.

Coop scarfed down the rest of his huge piece in about two bites. That guy could eat.

"You want any more?" he asked.

"Nope. Three pieces does it for me. You?"

"Naw. Let's go."

"What should we do with the rest?" Half a pizza sat in the box on the table.

"Just leave it," he said. "They'll come clean it up."

"They?" I asked. "Who?"

"I dunno. The cleaning people." He wiggled his fingers and made a *Twilight Zone* sound. "They're like Reginald. You never see them. They wait till you're out of a room before they come in. You never have to make your bed or pick your clothes off the floor. It's like—bing—magic. Everything's done for you."

"Oh," I said. This was weird. Nice, though. No chores. I could live with that. "How do they know when you're out of a room?"

"Big Brother, cuz. Big Brother."

"Huh?"

His light blue eyes crinkled along with the rest of his face as he smiled. "Cameras, my man. They're all over the place, taking in our every move."

Wait a minute. Our *every* move?

"There are cameras in here? Watching us right now?" I picked up a paper napkin and wiped it across my mouth.

"You catch on quick." He gave me a playful shove on the arm. "Maybe you really are smart enough to be a Top Floor."

"There isn't . . . there can't be cameras in the bathroom. And the closet? Do they watch us change our clothes . . . and do other things?"

81

"Don't sweat it," said Coop, picking a piece of pepperoni off the leftover pizza and shoving it into his mouth. "I freaked when I first found out too, but Miss Smoot told me they only monitor the bathroom and closet with audio equipment. It's one or the other— the video monitoring doesn't have audio and the audio monitoring doesn't have video. It's just to make sure we're safe. And they can't watch us twenty-four seven. There's like just a couple of dudes watching all five floors. They're not going to fixate on one dopey kid changing his socks."

"They better not."

"They won't."

A high-pitched electronic ring sent a few notes through my room. I sat up straight, clutching the arms of my chair.

"Doorbell," said Coop. "Must be your gym clothes." He got a wild, excited look in his eyes. "Ready for some paddle-wall-ball?"

"WHATEVER YOU DO, DON'T STEP FOOT in that room there."

Coop and I had just emerged from the gym, and he pointed straight down the wide space between the wall and the girls' cubicles to the room on the other side of the building.

I wiped sweat from my forehead with the back of my arm. The top floor was perfectly climate controlled, but Coop had given me a workout. I hadn't made it easy on him, either. Both of us had gone full-out for almost two hours; the only break was when we stopped to say, "No, we're not done with the gym," to a boy—Isaac, I learned—and a girl—Kia. They were both at least a year older than me. Isaac's pale skin turned red under his freckles and his cropped blond hair. He blasted us with a few rounds of his laser gun before stomping out of the gym. Kia—totally opposite-looking from Isaac with her smooth, dark skin and lots of hair spiraling down around her shoulders—retained her composure and lectured us for a few minutes about community property and the necessity of taking turns.

We still didn't let her have the gym.

I chugged my last gulps of water and let the plastic bottle slip out of my hand and thunk on the thick carpeting. According to Coop, our invisible maids would take care of it.

The two of us quickly approached the room Coop had warned me against. "What's so scary about it?"

"*They* have taken it over." He wiggled his finger at the deserted girls' cubicles as we walked past. "Turned it into a dance studio. Mirrors all over everything. And one of those ballet rails—you know? If they ever try to lure you in with the promise of a dance video tournament, run the other direction. It's not a game. They want to record you dancing with them. Like partners." His shudder made the ends of his hair tremble.

"Hey, whoa." I held out my hand, preventing Coop from entering the hallway to the boys' bedrooms. "Check it out." The sliding glass door to Reginald's cubicle stood open an inch.

"He's not in there anymore." Coop kept walking. "We'd better hurry. We've only got ten more minutes of light. I don't know about you, bro, but I *hate* changing clothes by flashlight."

"Hang on. I just want to look." Wow. Reginald had

quite the setup. Three monstrous monitors made a mini cubicle around the keyboards on the desk.

"I'm not messing with you. It's day one for you, so I know you haven't even thought about buying a light source yet. You don't know about the guards coming up and confiscating your lantern if you leave it on for more than a minute. You've never had to feel your way through your room before. Personally, I like to *see* what's on my toothbrush before I stick it in my mouth."

For some reason Reginald's cubicle seemed extra dark already. I looked up. The glass ceiling was covered with blinds as well. Was the guy allergic to light or something?

"I'm coming." I ran to catch up with Coop. He was right. This was only my first day on the top floor. I'd have plenty of chances to get the scoop on this mysterious Reginald guy.

I found Coop standing frozen outside the first door in the hall, his finger to his lips. "Dude, listen."

"Whose . . . is that Reginald's room?" It clicked. Reginald—first cubicle, first room. Me—fifth cubicle, fifth room. It only took me what—three hours to figure out? They were going to drop-kick me off the top floor if I didn't start catching on to things a lot faster around here.

"He's in there." Hitching his thumb, Coop tapped

Reginald's door. A soft, constant, metallic clanging noise made it through that heavy top-floor bedroom door.

"What's he doing?" I asked.

"Beats me." Coop's wide, goofy smile wiggled around his face. "I dare you."

My eyebrows arched high. "To . . ."

"Find out whatever you need to know, man. Get answers to all your questions." He made circles in the air in front of my face with his index finger. Slowly he lowered the finger.

"Coop, what are you . . . No!"

He pressed the finger firmly against the neon-green rectangle of light on the wall right next to the doorknob. Before I could suck in my next breath, he zipped back through the door to the cubicle area and out of sight.

"Coop!" I whispered my scream, knowing it wouldn't do any better if I bellowed it. One loud metallic clunk came from inside the room and then silence. I twisted to look way down the hall, to my bedroom. Nope, I'd never make it. Follow Coop? Maybe I could make that. Heavy footsteps pounded toward the door. I glanced up, wondering where the security cameras were. What kind of punishment would a Top Floor get for doorbell ditching?

"Who is it?" The voice coming through the door was very deep. This Reginald guy must be old. Sixteen or seventeen, maybe.

"I . . . uh . . . I'm Matthew Dunston. Um, you know . . . I'm new to the top floor and I thought it would be nice to meet everyone." Rolling my eyes, I shook my head in disgust at how wimpy and high-pitched my voice had come out.

"Oh." Long pause. "Hi."

"Hi."

Silence. Awkward, eternal silence. Isn't it a normal reaction for people to open the door when someone rings the bell? I may have been the newest newbie on the top floor, but I was getting the picture pretty darn clearly that Reginald was not your typical "normal" person.

"Well, I guess I'll see you around," I said.

"No."

No?

"How's it going, dude?" Coop had sneaked back into the hall. "No Reginald sighting yet, huh?"

"I'm working on it," I whispered back to him. "So, Reginald, we . . . uh, were just wondering if you want to see this . . . cool thing Coop has."

Coop's eyes bugged out, and his mouth dropped open, forming the word *What?*

"We'll think of something," I whispered.

"Can't," came Reginald's deep voice.

"Sure you can," I said. "We still have a few minutes until lights-out. Just open the door." 87

"Go away now." A few seconds later the metallic clanking started up again.

Coop and I kept our ears pressed to the door.

"Maybe he's building something," I said.

"Right," Coop deadpanned. "He must have an anvil in there. Do you think he's making a suit of armor?"

Three musical dings reverberated throughout the hallway—the five-minutes-until-lights-out warning.

We headed toward our rooms.

"No, wait," I said. "I've got it. He's chipping away at his wall. He's trying to break out."

"Yeah, right." Coop's hair flopped around his head as he laughed. "Like he'd want to do that."

The door between Coop's and Isaac's opened, and Jeffery poked his head into the hall. "I hope you two best buddies had a *great* time. You couldn't come close to how much fun I had. I'm halfway finished with my LEGO sculpture of an electron microscope. Oh! Another delivery."

He bent down and scooped up the two boxes that were sitting on the floor outside his door and disappeared back inside his room.

"Time's almost up. Tomorrow, dude." Coop hustled into his own room.

I made my way alone to the second to last door. My room.

I'd only gotten as far as putting on my pajama bottoms before—just as Coop had warned me—all the lights in my room began to fade. I glanced at my watch. Yep. Ten o'clock on the dot.

Coop was wrong about one thing. Brushing your teeth in the dark isn't so bad.

My eyes popped open. The clock on the nightstand told me it was just after one in the morning. The clock was neon-green, instead of red like the one at home. It took me a minute to remember where I was.

I sprang out of bed. Shoot. I'd let it slip my mind. What time was it again? Too late for a live contact. I'd meant to try to call—if I could ever get a signal—or e-mail my parents and Brennan and Lester before I went to bed. This top floor had a way of distracting you.

Ouch! I stubbed my toe on the leg of one of the table chairs as I felt my way to the closet. Overcorrecting to make sure I cleared the rest of the table, I crashed into the sofa. *Okay. Slow down. The end of the sofa is*—I slid my hands across the back of it until it dropped off—*here, so the closet is to my left—forward and at an angle. Nothing else there to trip over, if I remember right.*

I hadn't remembered I'd dumped my gym shoes outside the closet, and I stumbled over them. Forget groping around in the dark. Coop had to be wrong. 89

There *had* to be a way to get light in the middle of the night. What if some kid got sick? I found the wall and slid my hand along it, feeling for a light switch. There weren't any.

Eventually, I made my way to the big walk-in closet. I found my jeans right off—underneath my sweaty gym clothes—since they were one of the few items of clothing in there and I'd dumped them right in the middle of the floor. The other clothes I owned—the pajamas I'd ordered the night before and the clothes I'd worn to the workhouse—had magically morphed from a dirty pile in my room on the first floor into neatly washed, ironed, and folded bundles I found sitting on the wide shelves of my top floor closet when I first arrived. Even my boxers had been ironed. Talk about freaky. Made me consider throwing out my dirty underwear and ordering a new pair each day.

My cell phone was easy enough to find in the front pocket of my jeans. Still no signal. Sheesh. You'd think this building was in the back of a cave, or buried a hundred feet underground or something. The phone wouldn't have lasted long, anyway, since I'd left the charger at home. It did put off enough of a glow to help me find my way to the computer sitting on the desk next to the door.

The computer wouldn't turn on either—shut down

for the night like all the lights. Grumbling, I slumped back to bed, where I tossed and turned for what seemed like hours.

First thing in the morning I shot off some e-mails to Brennan, Lester, Mom and Dad, Nana—wondering what ever happened with the broken ankle situation since the limit crisis sort of took over—and, at the last minute, Lauren.

It's a race, I said to them, even though they couldn't hear. *Let's see which one of you is the first to write back.* My bet was on Brennan. He lived on the computer almost as much as I did.

No one won. Not a single person wrote back the next day.

Or the next.

I received messages from Honey Lady, and I sent out more messages to my family and friends.

By day three I knew there was a problem with the network or the programming or something. The people on the outside might have gone a day or two without answering me, but three? No way. I sent a message to Honey Lady:

> I'm not getting any e-mail from outside the
> workhouse. I can't connect to any chat sites.
> What's the problem?

She answered me later that evening:

That is strange. No one else has complained
about having troubles like this. Are you sure the
problem is on our end? Some people just don't
like to write. Either way, I'll have one of our tech
people look into it.

I'd wanted to blame the silence on a computer problem, but Honey Lady's response put an irritating grain
of an idea into my brain. What if my family and friends
really weren't writing to me? What if they were beginning to forget all about me and were going on with their
lives like I didn't exist anymore? I could disappear in this
workhouse, and no one outside would even care.

EIGHT A.M. TIME FOR SCHOOL.

I headed out my bedroom door, my stomach full and satisfied. Biscuits and gravy. Who'd have guessed a warm breakfast could taste so good? Mom was a fantastic cook, especially when our oven worked, but she wasn't much of a morning person. The most she ever did to prepare breakfast was point the way to the cereal cupboard.

I'd been experimenting for two weeks now. Every day since I'd arrived at the FDRA workhouse, I'd tried something new and exciting for breakfast. Belgian waffles with strawberries and cream. Breakfast burritos. Stuffed crepes. French toast. Blueberry pancakes. And lots of eggs with bacon or sausage.

I'd probably weigh three hundred pounds by now if Coop didn't keep me running around the paddle-wall-ball court or swimming every second after work.

"Hey, Coop," I said as I shut my door behind me.

"Hey, bro." We didn't have anything else to say to each other. Nothing new to report since we split up last night ten minutes before lights-out. I'd gotten good at my timing so I wouldn't have to get ready for bed in the dark anymore.

"More boxes." I nodded my head at the one large and two small boxes sitting outside Jeffery's door.

"Things never change much on the top floor," said Coop.

Jeffery's door flew open. The moment he saw us, his entire face soured.

"What's the delivery today?" I asked, pretending the two of us had ever had a civil conversation together.

"Like you even care," he said, scooping up the small boxes. "You can't blame a guy for trying to fill up the long, boring hours he has to spend by himself each night because *someone* came along and stole his only friend."

Coop reached out and clamped a playful hand on his shoulder. "Hey, little dude, call a time-out."

"Jeff, you know you're always welcome to join us for paddle-wall-ball. Anytime."

He glared at me, squinting his eyes until they were almost completely closed. "It's *Jeffery*." Ugh. I knew that. He'd told me at least a dozen times over the past two weeks. I just couldn't get used to using such a formal name on a twelve-year-old kid.

"Sorry."

He dumped the small boxes inside his room and

moved on to pushing the larger one through his door-way, since it was too heavy to pick up.

"And just what would the two of you do with me if I showed up in the middle of your precious paddle-wall-ball game? Use me as a target? Gee, I can't think of anything I'd rather do."

"Fine. Be like that. See if we ever try to be nice to you again." I nudged Coop, and the two of us headed down the hall.

"Sorry, little Jeffery man, I really do like hanging with you when you're not teed off at me." Pausing in front of the last door before the hallway ended, Coop put one finger to his mouth.

"Is he in there?" I whispered.

"Don't think so, but we can try. Just to be sure." With his goofy grin plastered on his face, Coop started pounding on Reginald's door and ringing the bell over and over again.

"Forget it." I headed into the cubicle area. "We're never going to get out here before he does. See?" I threw an arm toward the glass cube, the sliding door securely closed. I even risked a visit from a security guard by tug-ging on the handle. Locked. "He must wake up at like, four in the morning to make sure he beats everyone else."

"We'll get him someday," said Coop.

"You bet we will—it just won't be in the morning."

We reached Coop's cubicle. As he was about to begin his daily ritual of shooting free throws with his Nerf ball and hoop before sitting down to his computer, I snatched the ball and swooshed it through myself.

"Bro!" He swiped the ball off the floor, and I slipped around the wall into my cubicle.

Time for my own morning ritual.

Shoot! They still hadn't fixed the problem with my e-mail. The only item in my in-box was Honey Lady's daily motivational, rah-rah message. I didn't even read them anymore. They were always sappy sayings, like, *Learn to LOVE to work HARD, and you will discover that it is not HARD to WORK. The person who remains down once he falls ends up with nothing but a mouthful of mud. The slothful and lazy not only lose the game—they lose at life.* Whatever.

I sent Honey Lady what was turning out to be my daily message to her: *PLEASE FIX MY E-MAIL!!!*

Two weeks and nothing. After two *days* I started wondering if she was ignoring my requests on purpose. Since I also couldn't make calls on my phone, I began to think she was trying to cut us workhouse kids off from the outside—why she would do this, I had no idea. Then I asked some of the other Top Floors, and every one of them said they had no problem getting their outside e-mail. Good-bye, conspiracy theory. I was stuck with plain old boring technical difficulties. I knew Honey Lady was busy, but how long would it take for her to send a message to a tech support person? *Just fix it already, Honey Lady!*

"Ta-da!" The gloating, high-pitched voice floated over all the cubicles.

"Not again," I moaned.

"Hey, man, get used to it," Coop called from his side of our shared cubicle wall.

It'd happened every day since I arrived. Each morning Madeline made a grand entrance and strutted around like she was the coolest, best-looking thing alive. She actually thought we cared.

"Today's outfit is a VonClossen creation," she announced. "Notice the beadwork on this cord belt." What she called a belt looked like ten red cords with various beads stuck here and there. The end of it hung practically to her knees. I don't know why she was wearing that belt, but it definitely wasn't to hold up her pants. On top she wore a white shirt covered by a red shirt covered by a white jacket. I'd sweat under that many clothes. "I found the VonClossen website when I noticed the company's stock had doubled in the last nine months. I'm happy, and my clients are happy!" She threw her arms in the air and froze in a one-hip-forward pose right at the opening of my cubicle.

I gave her a weak smile and a nod as she continued on her course around the cubicles, pausing to turn and pose a few more times.

"It never ends?" I called to Coop. "Just how big is her closet?"

"Same size as yours." She'd retreated to stick her sneering face back in my cubicle. "Some of us know how to organize our wardrobes better than others."

"Some of us don't care!"

With a huff and a nose-in-the-air, hair-flipping turn, she strutted away.

Two seconds later screams of delight shot over the top of the cubicles. Neela and Paige were getting their first glimpses of today's fashion statement. Their high-pitched squeals grated on my ears like a painful whistle to a dog.

"Shut up, already!" Kia's response was as predictable as Madeline's daily show.

With or without Kia's warning I knew everyone would settle down within the next few seconds and get going on their four hours of computerized school-work. We would've done it even without the threat of a guard watching on the monitor and coming up to crack down on us. I don't care who you are—whether you're a model wannabe, a paddle-wall-ball fanatic, or an Indian princess—if you're smart enough to be a Top Floor, you've got enough nerd in you to love the challenge of ripping through the assignments that pop up on your screen and seeing how close to a perfect score you can get. I was actually *learning* something when I didn't have to wait for days on end until everyone else in the class caught on. The computer science projects I got on the top floor stretched me beyond anything available at my middle school. What I loved most were the math lessons. They taught me new theories and strategies. And an added bonus to computerized learning—I never had to eat school lunch.

I rubbed my hands together. *Come on, Mr. Computer Teacher, let's see if you've got anything worthy of my brain today.*

Five p.m. Free time.

Already? The paying work I did in the afternoon was hard, but that made it all the more satisfying when I clawed my way through it. They had me doing math modeling. Two days ago I'd finished a mathematical model for a marketing company, to predict how consumers would react under a specific situation. My current project was for a chemical company, to optimize one part of the process for manufacturing a certain type of plastic.

I'd get so into my work—fascinated by the way I could manipulate numbers and equations—I'd lose all track of time. Usually Coop peeked around the edge of the cubicle to call me to paddle-wall-ball before I had any idea it was close to quitting time.

It happened again.

"Let's hit the court, cuz," he said.

"Hold up. I've almost figured out this part."

"Five o'clock, man. You gotta shut it down or the feds'll come here and quote codes and laws at us till our ears bleed."

"Reginald always works longer. He works all the time."

"What makes you think that? You've got X-ray eyes now and can see through those closed blinds of his?"

I didn't have to answer, but I did anyway. "No."

"Free time, fool. It means you're free to do what you want. If your pants aren't itching after sitting eight hours a day pounding on a computer and you want to goof around on the Internet or play some games or invent a new programming language just for the fun of it, then free time says you're free to do it."

"He's not working overtime?"

"Not allowed. Go in and see for yourself if you don't believe me."

"No, I believe you," I said fast. Go in there? Disturb Reginald? Unthinkable. Besides, Gorilla Man or one of the other guards—who all looked so much alike from the neck down they could've been clones—would come and grab me if I even knocked on that glass door of his.

I typed in a few more keystrokes.

"I hate this! I'm never going to get it right!" The voice blasted from several cubicles down and carried throughout the entire room. It sounded like Neela, but I couldn't be totally positive, since none of the girls ever spent much time talking to me. A pounding noise followed from the same direction that sounded like the girl slamming her fists into her keyboard.

"Forget about it for today." This snooty voice I recognized. Madeline. "Come on. Let's go order dinner. Paige, log off now! What's with you two today?"

"Just a minute," Paige called back from her own cubicle.

"I can't quit. I can't!" Neela's wailing voice cried.

"You guys know they don't pay you extra for working overtime," said Madeline. Her voice moved from over by Neela's cubicle, the first girls' cubicle across from Reginald's, to Paige's cubicle, across from Coop's, and back again. "You're going to make the guards come up here, and you know how smelly they can be. How can you even stand that programming stuff, Paige?"

"I've almost got this," said Paige.

"Well I don't, and my deadline was three days ago! Miss Smoot is going to kill me. I just. Can't. Get. It!" 101

I logged off my computer and smirked at Coop. "Always a drama, huh."

He nodded. "With girls around. Come on, man." He practically dragged me out of my cubicle. "As much as I love designing databases—and I do, don't get me wrong—I gotta move. Now. Let's hit the court."

"Check that."

The voice startled us and made us look around. We'd passed Jeffery's cubicle—which he'd already vacated—and made it as far as Isaac's, but the voice belonged to Kia.

"Isaac, tell the little boys you and I have dibs on the court today," she said. It took us a few seconds to find her—well, her head anyway. She was standing on something, her desk or a chair maybe, so her black curly hair and dark face stuck over the top of the middle cubicle wall. I wondered if she often talked to Isaac that way. I also wondered if Reginald ever opened his ceiling blinds and if Kia had gotten a peek at him. Not likely.

"We have dibs on the court today, little boys," said Isaac, leaning back in his chair with his feet propped on his desk. He held a model spaceship and kept his eyes on it as he twisted it slowly in his hands. "Like it?" he asked, holding it up for Coop and me to admire—although we didn't. I really couldn't see much difference between the model he was holding and the dozens of others that crowded his desk and shelves. It was a miracle the guy could still fit his computer in that sci-fi collector's shop—although the computer was covered with aliens too. "I just got this one today. You know what it is?"

"No, and we don't care," said Coop. "You can't dibs the court. It's first come, first served. Always has been. And since Isaac is busy playing with his little toys, Matt and I are going to get there first."

"Sorry to crash your hard drive," said Kia. "I already talked to Miss Smoot about how you hog the court all the time with your stupid paddle-wall-ball game."

"And what would you choose to play in there? Something lame like basketball or volleyball?" Coop made his voice go up about two octaves. "Oh, Isaac, will you make that shot for me? I think I need to file my nails."

She didn't flinch. "You are so lame. Miss Smoot said I could write a sign-up schedule, which I did last night. I e-mailed a copy to everyone first thing this morning. Didn't you read it?"

Oops. I guess I'd deleted it, thinking it was an extra rah-rah message from Honey Lady. It must have been the message that had "Top Floor Cooperation" in the subject line.

"I have better ways to waste my time than reading e-mail from lowly animators like you two," Coop said, nudging me with his elbow.

Kia rolled her eyes and stuck her chin in the air. "It doesn't matter if you read it or not. Isaac and I are signed up for the gym from five fifteen until eight."

"It's the only room we can totally black out." Isaac sat up straight, getting excited. "We're making a movie with all these laser special effects. There will be tons of spaceships flying everywhere, and battles. It's going to be awesome. It's got everything."

"Yeah? How about a plot? Has it got one of those?" asked Coop with a sneer.

"Of course it does," said Kia from above.

"Hey, you know what? You don't need the gym." Coop was getting excited himself. "The girls' dance room doesn't have windows. You can use it!"

A high-pitched shriek came from the other side of the cubicles. Ten seconds later Madeline raced around.

"No way," she said, twirling the long red cords of her belt like a cowboy's lasso. "They are not allowed to use our dance room."

Coop was twitching all over the place, his muscles itching to get moving. I was anxious to get going too.

"Why not?" Coop asked. "You aren't using it. You don't own it!"

"Isaac, just how are you going to make your little spaceships fly for your movie?" Madeline asked, crossing her arms across the layers of clothing covering her chest.

"Wires. Gravity," Isaac said. "We'll throw a few, to see how that looks on film."

"See?" said Madeline, her stuck-up nose all crinkled. "Flying toys are not allowed in our dance room."

Coop's hands clenched into fists. *Easy there, bud. Hitting girls is not cool.*

He was able to keep his anger under control. "Give me one good reason."

"You're such a dunce, I don't know how you ever made top floor," she said. "The walls in there are covered with mirrors. Flying spaceships and mirrors don't mix."

"We can't use a room covered with mirrors anyway," said Kia. "The reflection would mess up all our shots."

"But . . . but . . ." Coop's hair flipped into his face as he jerked his head, searching the room for the solution that didn't exist.

"Bye-bye, little boys," said Kia as her head dropped out of sight.

"Bye-bye." Madeline waved, scrunched up her nose, and gave us a fake smile. Her voice deepened into a growl. "Neela! Paige! Now!"

"Just a minute!" The duet of girls' voices cried out.

"Fine. I'll just go make movie magic with Isaac and Kia."

"You will?" Isaac popped up in his chair, gripping the armrests. I couldn't tell if he was excited or terrified. 105

"No, she won't." Kia sauntered up to the group gathering outside Isaac's cubicle.

Madeline rolled her eyes dramatically. "Okay. Fine."

"I'm finished." Paige appeared at the edge of the row of cubicles. She pointed back toward the girls' side. "But something's wrong with Neela."

All six of us, every Top Floor except Reginald and Jeffery, rushed around to the girls' side. Neela was sitting at her desk, her head cradled in her hands and her shoulders shaking.

"Neela?" Madeline said. None of us dared cross through the invisible door and into the cubicle.

"I can't do it," Neela sobbed. Turning with her chair, she looked up and noticed the large group that had assembled.

"Are you okay?" I asked.

"No." She wiped at the tears streaming down her face.

"You should just knock off for today," I said. "Sleep on it. Let your subconscious work out the problems while you sleep. It works all the time for me when I'm stuck in the middle of a killer calculus problem. Just make sure you leave a pen, paper, and flashlight close to your bed so you can write down the answer when it comes to you in the middle of the night."

"I guess that's as good as anything else I've tried."

She jabbed the button that logged her off. "Thanks, Matt." She smiled a little, and then winced, squeezing her eyes together tight. "Madeline, you and Paige go on without me. I've got a really bad headache. I think I'm just going to go to my room and lie down."

"A headache? Again?" Madeline sighed. "Take some ibuprofen and get over it already."

"I have." Neela winced, as if something sharp had just jabbed her from inside her brain. Slowly, she pushed herself out of her chair. She started crying harder. "This one is the worst ever. Excuse me."

We moved aside as Neela passed through us and groped her way the short distance to the girls' hall.

"We should e-mail Hon—Miss Smoot," I said. "Neela needs a doctor or something."

"She's going to her room," said Madeline. "They'll monitor her condition while she's in there and come get her if she really needs it. *I* think she's being a drama queen over such a little headache."

I'm not buying that, I thought as the group broke up. Neela was in real pain. Headaches.

That was it. Tonight I would split from Coop an hour before lights-out and go data collecting. Time to put my hacking skills to use and figure out what was really going on here.

CHAPTER 11

SINCE THE GYM WAS OUT, WE ENDED up in the pool.

Coop let out a whoop as he ran the length of the diving board and gave it a big bounce.

"Cannonball!" he yelled, tucking his knees tight to his chest. He got some good air, then broke the surface of the water with a giant splash. Waves rippled out from where he landed and ran the length of the pool, reaching Jeffery at the other end. Jeffery was kneeling on a big, round, inflatable floating island. He looked up to glare at Coop's bobbing head until it went back under.

My turn. I decided to go for style instead of air and added a flip to my jump.

Swhoomp.

The water enveloped me. By the time I came back up, Coop had swum down by Jeffery and busied himself torturing the poor kid. Coop twirled the floating island around in circles while Jeffery tried to splash him with a paddle. I dove underwater and dolphin-swam half the length of the pool. Without surfacing, I grabbed Coop's legs and yanked him under.

He fought back. Jeffery splashed us with his paddle from on top of his island, but soon we pulled him in too. The three of us dunked, wrestled, and splashed one another until Jeffery called for mercy.

With the battle over, Coop swam to the deep end and did chin-ups off the edge of the diving board. Jeffery found his paddle, climbed out of the pool, and jumped back on his island. The island was so big he could've lain on his back with his arms and legs spread-eagled and still not have touched the edges. He paddled furiously but only succeeded in spinning himself in circles.

"I haven't seen this before." I gave the island a push in the opposite direction.

"It's new." He paddled harder, to make up for my push, I guess. He rose tall on his knees and wobbled as he tried to keep his balance.

Leaning my elbows on the edge of the thick island, I went along for the slow, spinning ride. "Hey, you know what would be fun?"

"If you left me alone?" he asked with plenty of venom.

"No, really. Let me show you." Swinging one leg over the top, I clawed my way up. My side of the island sank into the water, but it was so thick the top edge never came close to getting wet. The jostling sent Jeffery over the edge and into the water.

"Oops. Sorry," I said when his snarling face emerged. "Check this out, though." I staggered to my feet, my arms flapping to keep my balance.

"Go, bro!" Coop's loud voice echoed through the large space, coming from the top of the slide. "You're still lame compared to me!" He pushed off and down the twisting slide, headfirst and on his back.

A shock of cold shot through my body as a wet hand latched onto my ankle.

"Get off!" Jeffery yelled. Balance instantly became more of a challenge.

"Hi-yah!" Coop burst out of the water, heaving the top half of his body onto the island and grabbing my other leg.

Yeah, this was getting interesting.

"Whoa! Hey!" The struggle lasted a total of five seconds, ending with me in the water. By the time I came up for air, Jeffery had reclaimed his island, standing tall like I had and holding his paddle in front of him like a sword.

If only I had an island and a paddle of my own, I'd take Jeffery on. Hey . . . that could be fun.

I made the other two shut up for a minute and told them my idea. It would be like jousting on water—with two islands, two paddles, and two guys going at it.

"That could hurt," Jeffery said, rubbing his arm as if he'd already been smacked.

"Suck it up, little cuz," said Coop.

"We could pad the paddles—with blankets or something," I said.

Jeffery's eyes lit up. I could tell because he didn't wear his glasses in the pool. "A kayak paddle," he said.

"Yeah!" I said. "Padded on both ends. This is going to be awesome!"

Jeffery bounced on his island, like a little kid ready to go see what Santa had left in his stocking. "Can I figure out the padding? I'll buy all the blankets and rope or whatever. I'll take care of it all. Can I?"

Coop and I struggled to keep from bursting out laughing at his enthusiasm.

"Sure," I said.

"More boxes, Jeffery," I said as the three of us walked down the hall to our rooms. None of us had felt like staying in the pool. It wouldn't be any fun until our jousting equipment arrived.

He opened his door and kicked the small boxes inside.

"Careful!" I said. "It looks like electronics."

Jeffery's glasses kept slipping down his wet nose, and he had to constantly push them back up. "You guys

111

be sure to order express delivery. Okay? Overnight, if you can."

"Okay, bro," said Coop, opening his door.

Jeffery's door closed behind him. Before I got to my door, Jeffery's opened again. "Don't forget!"

"We won't!" I said.

"Chill, dude. We're Top Floors, you know. I think we can remember." Coop slipped inside his room.

With water dripping from my hair down my shoulders and back, my fingers flew over my keyboard. In less than a minute I'd located a site that sold islands like Jeffery's. I'd volunteered to order the second island, and Coop was in charge of getting two kayak paddles. I scrolled around and found an island in black and red—warrior colors. I was going to cream the poor little guy and his sky-blue and white island.

As I punched keys to complete the order, a laser shot out and scanned my eye. Just part of the process. It happened every day when I ordered my meals. It identified me and let them know where to send the merchandise. *Oops. Almost forgot. Jeffery would have had a fit.* I clicked on the express-shipping icon.

A line of letters in fine blue print appeared on the bottom of the screen. *Be aware that an additional express shipping fee will be charged to your account.*

My next breath stuck in my throat. My account. My

family's account. That was the whole reason I was here, but I hadn't given it a second thought since I'd arrived on the top floor. I'd assumed the food and clothes I ordered were covered by the FDRA, like a complete room and board package. Until today I'd never ordered anything off any site other than the links on this workhouse's main page. The links connected us to stores and restaurants located close by, so we could get our clothes fast and our meals hot.

I'd never had a reason to order anything off-site before. I hadn't been able to think of anything I wanted that wasn't already provided for me here—we had all the latest video games and movies. We could set up the gym for any sport we felt like playing—although Coop always chose paddle-wall-ball. Any piece of sports equipment we could dream of was already stored in a long closet off the gym.

I clicked the button to accept the additional shipping charge. I'd been working hard here and deserved something for my efforts. I wouldn't go crazy, though. I wouldn't buy a ton of designer clothes or collectible spaceship models or massive amounts of electronics. I still wanted to go home. Eventually.

My fingers tapped the keyboard, too light to do anything. There was something else I was going to do today—what was it? Oh, yeah! Hack for the headache data. Once I downloaded it, I could whip up a statistical analysis. . . .

Bam! Bam! Bam!

"Dude, quick! Reginald is on the loose."

I flew out of my chair and practically ripped the door off its hinges.

Coop was already at the other end of the hall, pointing at the first bedroom. "It's open and dark inside, and he's not there!" I didn't even slow down when I got to him. "His cubie is empty too. I noticed when I went to check out the gym—to see if the loser space movie wrapped up early."

I only paused for half a second. He was right. The sliding glass door stood open wide.

We raced down the row of cubicles and burst into the pool room. Empty. Jeffery's island stood in a corner, propped against the wall. Not even a ripple disturbed the water.

Out of the pool room. Through the cubicle room. Into the gym.

"Ahhhhhh!" Kia's scream was so high and loud we actually winced and covered our ears. "What are you idiots doing?"

"You just messed up our big chase scene!" Isaac's footsteps thundered in the nearly pitch-black gym, closing in on us.

"Sorry," I said, backing through the doorway fast.

"Downshift already, man," said Coop.

"Hey, is Reginald in here with you?" I had to ask.

"Reginald?" That took Isaac by surprise and made him stop and think. Not for long, though. "Of course not, you black-hole brains! What's wrong with you? I'm going to blast you into the eighteenth sector!"

We closed the door and sprinted toward the other end of the floor.

"You gotta be kidding me," Coop said as I reached for the doorknob. "No way will I believe we'll find Reginald in the girls' dance room, wearing a tutu and standing on his tippy-toes."

I took a quick glance inside anyway. The lights were on, but nobody was dancing.

Next we did a quick scan of the rec room—Madeline was yakking Paige's head off as they painted their toenails and watched a movie. We circled the cubicles one more time. No Reginald anywhere.

"He's messing with us," I said as we checked every one of the boys' bedrooms, even mine and the empty one next to it. "Watching us and keeping himself just around the corner."

"The girls' rooms." Firm, determined lines hardened Coop's face. "It's the only possibility."

I looked up and around, imagining the gorilla guards   115 watching us that very moment. "We can't . . . can we?"

"Won't know until we try." He slapped me with the back of his hand and we took off. "We gotta be quick about it."

We weren't quick enough. We skipped Neela's room—first girls' cubicle, first girls' room—because we knew she was in there feeling sick. We'd just finished a quick peek into Kia's room and were heading toward Madeline's when two giant hands clamped down on our shoulders.

"Uh, hi?" I said, turning to look up into the angry eyes of a blond Gorilla Clone guard.

Without a word—but with lots of pressure on our shoulders—he turned us around and marched us out of that hall. Once in the cubicle room, he shoved us forward, making us stumble a few steps.

Coop and I headed back to our bedrooms, each of us rubbing a shoulder. We stopped short the second we stepped into the boys' hallway. Reginald's door was closed tight. From inside came that familiar, steady metallic clanging. Shoot. We should have at least taken a look inside his room when we'd had the chance.

Who was this guy? Was he for real? I was beginning to think he could move around the top floor without being detected, like a mist or a ghost. And what the heck was he doing in that room of his?

CHAPTER 12

SEVERAL TRAYS WITH NUMEROUS empty plates, covers, and utensils sat on the ground outside of Reginald's tightly sealed cubicle. I kicked them softly as I walked by. The wild goose chase he'd sent me on last night had made me forget about my hacking project until it was too close to lights-out.

The remnants of sausage, bacon, eggs—both scrambled and fried—and steak shifted on Reginald's breakfast plates, making me picture those trays coming in, overflowing with fat and protein. I shifted a few plates with my foot to get a better look. Man, this guy hadn't ordered a speck of granola or even one tiny grape. Just thinking about it made my stomach heavy.

"No!" A panicked female wail made me jump. "No, no, no!" My heart slowed back down fast. Sounded like Madeline. She'd probably just discovered her socks didn't perfectly match the rest of her outfit. "Where is she?" Madeline's voice took on a new level of fear and intensity as she burst into the cubicle room. "She can't be gone. It's not possible!"

Coop emerged from the hallway. "Hey, yo, bro, what's up?"

Shrugging, I followed him around to the girls' side. We found Madeline inside Neela's cubicle ripping open drawers and slamming them shut again. A white-faced Paige stood outside the cubicle, gripping the edge of the cloth-covered wall with both hands while she watched Madeline's fit and sobbing much quieter tears of her own.

"What's going on?" I asked. "Where's Neela?"

"That's just it." Madeline gave Neela's chair a kick that sent it crashing against the wall. "They took her. She's gone!"

"Gone where?" Once you get taken to the workhouse, is there anyplace else to go?

"I don't know," Madeline wailed.

"I just . . ." Paige, speaking in a much softer voice, paused to sniff. "I knocked on her door after breakfast . . . and she wasn't there."

"She came and got me right away, of course. And now look at this!" Madeline grabbed onto the back of Neela's chair and gave it a good shake. "They've emptied out her room and clean-swept her cubicle." She threw her arms out and stared at the ceiling, maybe looking into a security camera. "What have they done with her?"

"People come and go from the top floor all the time."

All of us froze. Honey Lady's smooth, calm voice behind us was not what we'd expected.

Madeline ran over and threw her arms around her. "Miss Smoot, where is she? What happened to her?"

Honey Lady gave Madeline's back three quick, efficient pats. "You're just witnessing FDO 169-D in action. The workhouse did exactly what it was supposed to do." She sprinkled her calm, confident words over our heads like powdered sugar. "You all know your work here is what will eventually get your families back under their limits and get you back home where you belong. Right?"

Sure we all knew that. We just didn't think about it much. It was kind of cool living here, on our own for the most part, our every wish granted with just the click of the mouse. Home would come . . . later.

"Neela has completed her time on the top floor," said Miss Smoot. "It's as simple as that. It just took you by surprise because this workhouse is only six months old. Neela is the first Top Floor to leave us."

Madeline untangled herself from Honey Lady, wearing a matching gushy smile. "Wow, she finished? Her family really got back under their limit? I mean, it just happened so fast."

"We don't feel the need to waste a lot of time here at the FDRA. Numbers are numbers. If you're over your   119 limit, you're over. As soon as you go under—even by a penny—you're under."

"Yeah, they sure didn't waste any time snatching me up after my mom went over the limit at the store," I grumbled under my breath to Coop. "And taking Neela like that in the middle of the night, without even letting her say good-bye . . ."

"I don't . . ."

The rest of us shut up, straining to hear the soft words coming from Paige. Words from her were an anomaly, so we all felt a compulsion to listen intently to the few she let slip out.

At everyone's rapt attention, the rest of her sentence got stuck in her throat.

"Yes, Paige?" Honey Lady nodded in a more subdued cheerleader mode. "Go on."

"I'm just surprised," Paige said, staring at her hand rubbing up and down the edge of the cubicle wall. "Neela told me why she had to come here—her parents develop real estate, and they sank millions into a project that went under. I mean . . . I guess I don't understand how her family could recover from that much debt so fast."

"A year and a half," Honey Lady said, staring into her handheld computer device. "Neela was one of the very first children to participate in FDO 169-D when it started one and a half years ago. She spent her first year at the northeast workhouse before being transferred to this one six months ago when we opened. I understand your confusion, Paige, but it just tells me that you don't fully comprehend the complexities of family debt limits or the volatile business of real estate development. You said yourself that her parents lost millions overnight. Doesn't it stand to reason that in their business it is also possible to *make* millions overnight?"

Pinching her lips together tightly, Paige nodded, looking away from Honey Lady. Paige wasn't convinced. Or maybe she just felt bad about losing a friend. I was bummed too. My chance to get to know the Indian princess had disappeared forever. Leave it to me to never have a conversation with a girl I kind of liked even when we were locked up on the top floor together.

I guess I should be glad for Neela, getting out of here and away from whatever it was that was giving kids headaches—if something in the workhouse really *was* giving kids headaches. Logically, I'd think more of us would be sick if some noxious cleaning product were floating around the air ducts. One kid—Neela—out of all nine of us on the top floor had started getting them. That didn't seem statistically significant. I needed more data—all of it, on the entire workhouse.

But how was it the one top-floor headache kid came

from a family who just happened to get under their limit first?

I don't like coincidences. Give me facts—some solid numbers I can analyze.

Tonight, for sure, I'd get that data and find out what—if anything—was going on around here.

CHAPTER 13

"NO, COOP, I GOTTA DO THIS. MAYBE if I get lucky and can get in fast, I'll meet up with you and Jeffery in the gym later."

"Bro, come on." I'd never heard Coop whine before. Turned out he was a pro.

"Later." I shut my bedroom door in his face.

Now to get hacking.

My fingers hung above the keyboard, unmoving. They used to just take off on their own. A thought would come to me of what I wanted to do, and then I'd set my fingers loose to take care of the details on their own. I think I was out of practice.

Closing my eyes, I imagined myself back in the computer room at home. I'd be sitting at the computer on the left side of the room, Lauren would be chatting online while texting or talking on her phone at the middle computer, and either Mom or Abbie would be at the computer against the right wall, shopping or playing.

Brennan, Lester, you guys there?

Yeah, we're here.

Ready to start hacking. What about you, Matt? You up for a tough one tonight? What should we try?

The school. I want to check my grades.

Lame, Lester. You can do that legally through the front door.

But it's fun to check them when you hack in. Come on, guys.

No. Too easy.

Shut it down for a minute, you two. I've got a big one to try. A government agency.

Ooooh, I'm shaking in my shoes. Let me at it.

I don't know. If we get caught, we could be in really big trouble.

It isn't a game this time. It's important. You guys with me?

With the imagined rousing cheers of my buddies thundering in my brain, I charged in. The world slipped away around me as I became absorbed in my work. My mind clicked and calculated, strategized and maneuvered. Slowly, steadily, I chipped away at the site's defenses. Besides the fluff files, like the guard-duty schedule and the cleaning-crew supply order forms, the workhouse's files were proving to be tough to crack into. It took me a while before I realized the meaty files were stored on a completely different site. The guys and I had never tried a government agency before. Security seemed to be their middle name. The lights started dimming around me.

What the heck?

I glanced at the clock in the bottom corner of the screen. How could it be so late already? Dang. My computer gave me a five-minute warning, and I worked furiously until it started closing itself down for the night.

The longest Brennan, Lester, and I had taken to hack in and retrieve any info we'd ever wanted was . . . what, a couple of days? But we'd never tried anything *really* tough. We used to race to see which of us could hack into some moderately secure place—like the school or one of our parents' computers at work or something— just for the fun of it. It wasn't for fun this time. It was for real. And I was going to do this, no matter how much Coop whined that he needed a paddle-wall-ball partner.

After three days of hacking, Coop was ready to burst a major artery. I couldn't stop, though, not for anything. I didn't even take the time to bother Honey Lady with reminders about my e-mail problem—which still hadn't been fixed.

My floating inflatable island had arrived. It sat—still in the box—in the bottom of my closet. At least Jeffery wasn't pounding on me to spend time with him jousting yet. Every day he showed Coop and me pencil sketches of his paddle-jousting-pole designs. He said he was on a quest to find the perfect design. Instead of wearing swimming trunks, Jeffery's warriors often had on full armor. One even sat on a horse. Jeffery had gone over the edge.

One of my hands left the keyboard for a minute to snatch a baby carrot out of the takeout container that held my dinner. I'd gone my whole first week on the top floor without eating a single vegetable—unless you count the onions on the hamburgers and pizzas. I'd actually started to miss the crunch. I'd been eating my veggies daily for a week and a half now. Mom and Nana would be proud.

Popping the entire carrot into my mouth, I looked up at my monitor.

"Hey!" The carrot slid to the back of my throat, making me cough it back up. "I got it! I got in!" Beaming and chewing, I half turned in my chair, expecting praise from . . . I don't know who. I turned back to the screen. "Let's see what we've got."

It didn't turn out to be much. Not the headache data I was looking for, anyway. I started exploring and found the info about the people on each floor. I clicked the top floor icon. Yep. There we were. Henry Cooper, Matthew Dunston. Everyone. Check it out—Brock Reginald. Reginald was his last name, not his first. And Brock—that made me think of a big linebacker or a heavyweight wrestler. Talk about a name that didn't match the person—or at least my imagined image of the person.

I also found info about our school curriculum and our current grades. I didn't see anything less than an A-minus for any of the Top Floor grades I checked—even for those of us working on some college-level classes. I found the current work assignments for each of us and—whoa—our pay scale. We were all pulling in pretty hefty hourly wages. And bonuses. I got one when I completed that math-modeling project for a traffic-flow analysis two days early. Cool. Poor Neela, though. I bet she never got any bonuses. And then I saw Reginald's numbers. Man, oh man. That brainiac was raking it in. I took a second look at what type of work he was doing to justify the big bucks. I couldn't even pronounce it. All I could tell was that it was something very scientific, complex, and advanced. They needed a whole new level of the top floor just for Reginald's brains.

I clicked on a marker under my name, and all my personal data popped up. Age, weight, health concerns—none, thanks—home address, parents' names, siblings, schools attended.

Back up. What was that under the siblings category, next to Lauren's name? It said *FDRA WH#MW 3rd Floor*.

My blood pulsed fast in my veins as I clicked on Lauren's name.

127

The information sent me and my chair sliding back from the desk, as if someone had punched me right in the chest. I grabbed the front of my shirt, my fingers making a tight fist around the handful of cloth.

Lauren Dunston

Age: 12

Parents: William and Rebecca Dunston

Assignment: 3rd Floor

Lauren was here. She'd arrived four days ago.

SLAMMING MY FISTS AGAINST THE
armrests of my chair, I jumped up. I
paced a full circle around my sofa and
back to the desk. How could Lauren
be here? What was going on at home? I shoved my
computer chair and then kicked it. What was wrong
with my parents that they could allow this to happen
to Lauren?

*She's right here, in this building. So close. I've got to
find her. I've got to get off this floor!*

Bursting out of my room, I bumped into Coop,
pacing the hall.

"Bro, you're done! Let's hit the gym."

I pushed past him. "Not now."

"Where are you going?"

"Third floor."

"No way, dude."

Waving him off, I raced toward the hallway to the
elevators. "Later, Coop."

"Dude, wait. When I say, 'no way you're going

down there,' I mean there's *no way* you're going to be able to *get* down there."

My hand clamped around the metal bar to the elevator hall door. "Why? Because I didn't fill out a stupid form? What are they going to do to stop me?"

With a loopy cock of his head and half a smile, he shrugged. "Go ahead, fool. Find out for yourself."

"Okay. Fine. I will." I slammed through that door and ran toward the elevator. "Matthew Dunston!" Not a ding or a swoosh of the doors sliding open. My palm slapped the bare wall next to the elevator. How did this thing work when I needed to go down?

With a final punch to the wall, I turned to the emergency stairs. The third floor was only two flights down. Probably faster than the elevator anyway. I pushed on the metal bar across the middle of the door, but nothing happened. Leaning my shoulder into the door, I pushed harder. What kind of emergency exit didn't let you into the stairwell? What did they expect us to do if the building caught on fire? We'd be trapped.

Or would we? I couldn't believe there was no emergency release system. Only one way to find out for sure. I ran out of the hall.

"We've got to start a fire, Coop." He'd vanished. I could just see him warming up with a few practice swings while he waited for me in the gym, thinking the elevator and locked door would make me give up. If so, he'd underestimated me.

I didn't really need his help anyway. As I headed to my room, my mind sorted through all the different ways to spark a flame. Flint and steel. Rubbing two sticks together. Focusing sunlight through a magnifying glass. I'd bet anything Jeffery owned a magnifying glass, but the sky was clouded over today. If only I had a packet of matches.

A memory popped into my head from a few days ago when Coop and I had looked into the rec room and seen Madeline and Paige painting their toenails. The girls had set up a dozen of those scented candles around them on the floor. The candles had been lit.

Doubling back, I ran toward the rec room. I did a quick search of the cupboards lining one wall. After several shelves full of board games, I hit pay dirt. I found the candles and a pink butane candle lighter. I clicked on the flame. Beautiful. But not very smoky.

I had to work fast. A gorilla guard could catch sight of me at any moment. I hustled to my cubicle, snatched up a piece of scratch paper, and crumpled it in my fist. When I touched the flame to a corner of the paper it caught but died out almost immediately. *Dang.* No, wait. The edges of the burned corner glowed bright orange as smoke drifted into the air. *Yes!* Smoke was what I was really after. I stuck the lighter into one of my desk drawers. Now, where was a smoke detector? I really should have thought this through more carefully.

A quick look up confirmed my suspicions that even if there had been a detector in this room, the ceiling was too high for my smoke to have reached it. I raced back to the elevator hall. There it was, right inside the door. Stretching as tall as I could, I held my smoky paper under the detector. *Come on.* Was I too low? Maybe the smoke needed to be closer. I'd have to run and get a chair. A gorilla guard was going to spot me before long for sure.

Beep! Beep! Beep! Beep! Beep!

Click.

My head snapped toward the emergency stairs door. I'd done it!

The noise from the smoke detector stopped as suddenly as it started. My small whiffs of smoke had dissipated fast. I hoped that didn't mean the door would immediately lock. I didn't hear anything. I raced to the door, hoping the system needed to be reset manually and I'd have time to get down to the third floor.

Yes! It was open. A smile tugged on the corners of my mouth as I smothered out the smoldering edge of the paper, shoved it in my pocket, and got my first look at the stairs. They went up one more floor—to the roof, I supposed—but that wasn't where I was headed. I ran down one set of stairs, turned, down another. Fourth floor. Down, turn . . . Footsteps. Pounding up. I practically jumped the entire last set of stairs to land me on the third floor. Another couple of steps got me out of the stairwell. The third-floor elevator hallway was identical to the one on the top floor. I sped through it and burst into what I expected to be a room the exact double of the top-floor cubicle room.

It wasn't.

I felt as if I'd stepped into a cave, from the contrast of the bright top floor with this dark, closed-in one. No skylights here—duh. Much lower ceilings, fluorescent lighting. No cubicles, either. Dozens of computers sat on long rows of sturdy wooden tables with a jumbled mess of power cords and cables spilling off the edges and pooling on the floor.

And the kids. They were all over the place. Lots of them. Groups of twos or threes stood together, talking and going in and out of doors. I would have just stood there staring for hours if I hadn't heard a clattering from the door behind me. I sprinted, straight across the floor.

"Lauren!" I called as I ran. "Lauren Dunston!" Two girls right in front of me stopped gabbing and stared at me with bugged-out eyes. "Do you know Lauren Dunston?"

One girl shook her head.

The other girl's eyebrows shot up. "Wait. She's new,

right?" Leaning to her friend, she said, "She's the one with major texting withdrawal. I think she's in her room. Do you want me to . . . hey! You're not allowed in there."

High, frantic girl voices tattling to one of the gorilla guards carried loud and clear to me. "Some weird boy just ran in here and went into the girls' hallway!"

I threw open the first door. "Lauren?"

No answer. Two bunk beds lined the walls of the room, which was the same size as mine. It took me a quarter of a second to calculate that the third floor could hold forty-eight kids. Man, that's a lot. Their rooms had no flat-screen TVs or—I glanced into the opening to the bathroom—nope, no heated towel racks or jetted tubs.

A low moan came from deep inside the room. I saw the form of a girl on a bottom bunk rise up to look at me. She had her hands pressed tightly to the sides of her head.

Headache.

"Sorry," I said, ducking out. I had to move faster. Next room. "Lauren?"

Nope, but another headache girl. She was kneeling on the sofa—much more shabby than the one in my room—with her head burrowed deep in the cushions, rocking herself back and forth.

"Hey!" The gorilla guard stood at the top of the hallway. He was the shortest of all the guards I'd seen, but his muscles were still intimidating. I took off in the opposite direction, to a dead end, but what choice did I have?

"Lauren!" I yelled as I ran. I'd almost reached the end of the hall when the last door opened. And there she was. *Of course, idiot.* She was the newest Third Floor. She'd be assigned the last room.

"Matt? Matt!" She rushed to me, about to smother me in a hug, but I had to keep moving. Gorilla Guard was closing in. I'd spied another door at the end of the hall. This door didn't exist in the back of the boys' hall on the top floor.

Grabbing Lauren by the wrist, I pulled her through the door. We stopped for two seconds to catch our breath and figure out where we were. It was another set of emergency stairs, situated in the opposite corner of the building from the set of stairs by the elevator; I was sure fire code required it. I figured my smoking paper had unlocked every emergency exit in the building. Good to know none of us would be trapped in a fire, but right now I was happy to use the stairs as a gorilla-guard escape route.

"Come on." I took the stairs up two at a time.

"Where are we going?" Lauren asked, stumbling behind me.

I tripped over a step. Good question.

135

"Matt. Stop. Why are we running?"

The door below us on the third floor exploded open, and Gorilla Twin stood there, huffing out loud breaths of air.

"We're running because he's chasing."

"Did you do something wrong?" she asked, wrenching her arm loose and stepping down one stair. "Because I didn't. I don't want to get into trouble."

"We're not doing anything wrong."

Gorilla Twin thundered up the few steps toward us.

"Leave us alone!" I yelled.

Gorilla Twin's giant hand clamped down on Lauren's shoulder. She shrugged him off as if he were a feather, lifting both hands up in a don't-touch-me pose.

"I don't want trouble. I'll go back to my floor."

He moved aside to let her pass back down the stairs. She opened the door, but before she stepped into the girls' hallway, she frowned up the stairs at me. "And, just so you know, Matt, I think you've been *very* rude. I *always* answer e-mails within a day at the most. Do you know how awful you're making Mom and Dad feel?" Right before she pranced through the doorway, she stuck her nose in the air and flipped her long hair. Mid-flip she froze, wincing. One hand lifted to the side of her head and pressed as she squeezed her eyes against the pain.

Lauren had a headache.

Long seconds passed as she moved in slo-mo through the door. The *ka-clunk* of its latches clamping together as it closed echoed up through the stairwell. Short Gorilla Twin and I locked eyes for an instant, and then I sprang into motion, turning and scrambling up the stairs.

"I'll go to my floor. I promise!"

The pounding footsteps kept coming, so I kept running. Survival instinct drove me through the first door I saw, which landed me on the fourth floor. Stupid. I don't know where I thought I could run or hide. I stood at the end of the fourth-floor girls' hallway and was met with shrieks and the slamming of doors. As I ran out of the hall, I did catch a glimpse inside one room. No bunk beds on this floor, but there were two beds to a room here.

A big group of kids stood at the end of the first row of cubicles, blocking the easy route I'd decided to take to the set of stairs by the elevator. Since there was no area in the workhouse I could really escape to, and since Lauren was finished talking to me for the day, I'd realized the only place for me to go was back to the top floor. Maybe if I locked myself in my room, Short Gorilla Twin wouldn't tear my arms off.

I took a quick left and ran down the row of girls' cubicles, circling the big room. I stumbled, but didn't stop, when I noticed that there were two rows of double cubicles on this floor and that, logically, they were each about half the size of ours on the top floor. No pool room here, either, which made sense if you thought about it. Our pool hung down and took up the space on this floor as well as on our own.

I turned the last cubicle corner, ready for a long straight sprint to the hallway, when I practically crashed into a group of girls. They didn't give me a second glance, but the sight of one of them made me slam on the brakes instead of zooming around them.

"Neela?"

The girl chatter died away fast as the entire group stopped and turned toward me.

"Is that you, Neela?"

"Oh, hi." She turned to the other girls. "This is a guy from the top floor. Matt. Did you get moved down too?"

I slowly shook my head from one side to the other.

"Maybe you should try to. It's tons of fun on the fourth floor. We're getting ready to have a dance in the rec room. We don't have a dance room here, but the rec room is twice as big. Fourth-floor boys aren't afraid to dance with us."

"Neela, what are you doing here? Miss Smoot said you went home."

She snorted out a laugh, which seemed strange coming from her delicate Indian-princess face. "Home? As if. My family is never getting under their limit. I had to accept that a long time ago."

"So how come . . . why did they make you move down? And in the middle of the night."

"Who knows why they do what they do?" Neela linked elbows with the two girls standing closest to her. "And I don't care what any Top Floor says. I *like* it down here. So what if we don't have a pool and our gym only converts from basketball to volleyball? I don't even care that I get paid less. The work is *so* much easier. Nobody is snobby, either."

One of the girls broke away. "Hey, Neela, I'm going to go to our room and call down for some meds. I want to feel better in plenty of time for the dance."

"Hey, yeah, will you get some for me, too? Low dose today. It's not too bad."

The corners of my mouth tugged down. Even as I heard the heavy clomp of Short Gorilla Twin's feet coming up behind me, I leaned in, almost whispering. "Why are you guys taking medicine? Are you . . . taking stuff you shouldn't?"

She waved me off. "Of course not. It's just a simple painkiller. No side effects at all. Safe enough to take every day—which I usually do—although it doesn't always help."

"What do you take it for?" As if I hadn't already figured that out.

She shrugged, unconcerned. "Headaches—from sitting at the computer so much. You know, the light from the monitor plus sitting and thinking so hard all day. Lots of kids get them."

"No one on the top floor gets headaches. Except . . . you."

The gorilla hand clamped around the back of my neck, and my short visit to the fourth floor came to an abrupt end.

CHAPTER 15

GORILLA TWIN'S GRIP ON THE BACK of my neck had so much muscle behind it he almost lifted me off the floor as he directed me to the elevator. He used a code instead of his name, and it opened right up for him. We didn't stop moving once we got to the top floor. He didn't release me to let me go find Coop, and he didn't let me save face by avoiding Paige and Madeline, who were taking a food delivery outside the rec room door.

Gorilla Twin marched me straight down the hall and into my bedroom, propelling me inside with a not-so-gentle push.

"Oh, uh, hi." I fought to regain my balance quickly. Honey Lady sat smiling on my sofa, those long legs of hers crossed and one arm stretched across the back. With a twitch of her head, she instructed me to sit by her.

"I heard you had a little adventure today." Her liquid-sugar voice poured out in a smooth stream.

Shrugging, I slumped into the other corner of the sofa. "Why did you lie to us about Neela?"

"What concerning Neela do you believe I lied about?"

"You said she went home."

Honey Lady's chin lifted in a big nod. "And you bumped into her on the fourth floor."

"Yes!"

She leaned far across the sofa, grabbing onto my thigh. The flowery scent came along with the rest of her. "It's tricky, you know? Neela's case was a tough one to call, but rules are rules. Her family was barely able to duck under their limit. Because of their financial history I suspected they'd used some soft accounting practices. When I told you she'd gone home, I sincerely hoped she'd be able to. She actually spent a day in the holding room on the first floor while we investigated the situation thoroughly. Unfortunately, it turned out that a property her parents claimed as an asset was grossly overvalued, and they were still over their limit. Neela was quite embarrassed, as you can imagine, and begged me to let her move to the fourth floor, so the rest of you Top Floors wouldn't find out about her situation. You won't tell the others about her, will you? She'd be devastated."

"Guess not," I mumbled, staring at my fingers. "My sister came here four days ago."

Honey Lady nodded. "I am aware of that."

"But you didn't think that maybe I'd like to know?" I

rose up straighter. "I want to see her—have a good long talk with her without being chased down."

"If you stay in your assigned area, none of our security personnel will ever pay you any notice."

"Before today nobody told me I was locked on the top floor."

One of her eyes closed halfway as she tilted her head to one side. "I thought I made it clear to you when you first arrived that you need to stay on your assigned floor. A lot of kids live in this workhouse, and I'm responsible for each and every one of you. Do you have any idea what a big job that is? The only way we can even begin to monitor you is if you are sorted out. Can you imagine the nightmare I'd have keeping track of everyone if you were all free to roam anywhere in the building? It's a matter of safety, as well as security and order." She gave my knee a slight squeeze, and her voice got peppier, even though a hint of a threat lay beneath it. "I have to follow fire codes, so the smoke alarm release must remain functional. I trust you understand how dangerous it can be for kids to leave their floors and that you won't try tripping it again. Don't force me to place extra monitoring on you."

I crammed myself farther into the corner of the sofa, pushing her hand off my leg. "I want to see Lauren."

Honey Lady didn't say anything for a moment as she slid her lips back and forth against each other.

"Why don't you write her a nice e-mail?"

"Why don't you fix my account?" I'd never spoken so rudely to an adult before. My patience with the whole e-mail problem had run out. "Lauren said they've been e-mailing me, but I haven't got one message from home yet."

"You're kidding! Matt, I'm so sorry. I hadn't heard anything from you about it in the last couple of days, so I assumed the problem had been taken care of. I'll get the tech team on it ASAP."

"Hang on," I said as I thought out loud. "Lauren is in the workhouse now, so I should be able to get her messages. But she's been here for four days, and I still haven't gotten any. That doesn't make any sense."

"You're right, it doesn't," said Honey Lady. "Are you sure she wrote to you during that time? Either way, I'll be sure to mention it to the tech team."

"I don't want to e-mail her, anyway. She's here. I want to talk to her face-to-face."

Several long seconds passed before she finally said, "I suppose that can be arranged."

"What's there to arrange? All I need to do is walk down to the third floor. Or Lauren can come up here."

Honey Lady shook her head and opened her mouth.

I spoke before she had the chance to shut me down.

"I want to go now."

"Of course you do." She reached out to squeeze my thigh again, but her hand froze before it got there, her fingers contracted, and she pulled back. "Listen, Matt, I think it's a great idea for you to have a visit with your sister. I just need to think how to best accomplish that. We can't let the other Top Floors and Third Floors see you and Lauren wandering around on floors other than your own." Rising to her feet, she gave my shoulder a quick pat. "Tell you what, I'll figure something out and let you know soon. All right?"

"I want to see her tomorrow."

"That might be pushing—"

"Tomorrow, or you're going to have one heck of a time keeping me on this floor."

One corner of her closed mouth lifted. "You think so? Interesting. I wouldn't be too anxious to test that theory if I were you. Life on the top floor can be as pleasant . . . or as miserable as you choose to make it. I'll get back to you about your sister."

I clenched my teeth to keep my chin still as she walked out of my room. *No, Honey Lady, don't* you *be too anxious to test* me.

All through the next day my mind wandered away from my computer screen and down to Lauren on the third floor. I comprehended zero of my history reading assignment and even missed a calculus problem. Every hour on the hour I sent Honey Lady an e-mail reminding her to contact me. She never wrote back. As the last minutes of lunch break ticked away, I scribbled a message on a piece of paper in thick black marker that said, *Contact me, Ms. Smoot!* Standing on a chair, I held the paper high in the air and moved it slowly from side to side, so one of the security cameras would be sure to pick it up.

My work couldn't suck me in. I kept glancing at the clock in the lower corner of my screen, grinding my teeth when the numbers didn't change fast enough.

With one minute to go I checked my in-box again. Still nothing from Honey Lady.

"Ready, Matt?" Her voice made me jump and spin around. She stood at the opening of my cubicle.

"Where's Lauren?" I asked.

"She's meeting us in the lobby."

"Let's go!" I sprang out of my chair, sending it sliding to crash against my desk.

It was all I could do to keep from running. Even walking, I still beat Honey Lady to the elevator by a good ten seconds.

"Sharlene Smoot, first floor," she said, strong and clear. It opened for her as easily as it had for the gorilla guard.

The elevator carried us down, not moving nearly fast enough. I bounced on my feet, thinking I should have started another fire and taken the stairs. Finally, the elevator came to a stop with a little bump. The instant the doors slid open, I burst through them and sprinted into the lobby. Other than Crab Woman hunched over her computer at her desk, not a single person occupied the space. I walked around the chairs and sofas, as if Lauren might be crouched behind one of them.

"Where is she?" I asked.

"Just wait," said Honey Lady with that sweet smile of hers. She settled into one of the chairs, crossing her long legs. They distracted me for a second.

"Matt!"

The next thing I knew, Lauren threw herself against me, practically knocking me over. Her arms wrapped around my neck and squeezed so tight I couldn't breathe. For a moment I made do without air.

I nudged her softly to loosen her arms. "You . . . you're not mad at me anymore?"

"Of course not. I don't know why I said that stuff last night. We were just worried about you, since you never write back to us."

"I wrote you guys a lot, but something's wrong with my account. I've never received a single e-mail from home."

147

"Lauren and Matt, come sit down. You'll be more comfortable." Honey Lady stood up, grabbed on to Lauren, and guided her to a seat on the sofa closest to the chair she'd chosen for herself. "Matt, why don't you tell Lauren about the projects you've been working on since you arrived."

"She hates when I talk math," I said, sitting down close to my sister.

"You got that right," she said, snuggling up to me. "My work is weird. I mean, I don't even know how to do it. Still, I have to sit in my little chair and stare at the computer screen for four hours every day. It's really stupid."

"You're still in the training period," said Honey Lady. Leaning around Lauren, she told me very forcefully, "I assure you, your little sister is *not* just sitting in a chair and staring at her computer screen."

Lauren shrugged. "That's what it seems like."

At that moment I couldn't have cared less about Lauren's boring work assignment. "Tell me what's going on at home. How is it possible that you ended up here? Can you think of anything Mom and Dad have been doing different with their money?"

"I don't know," said Lauren. "I mean, I didn't notice anything—well, besides the new car. Dad didn't want to buy it, but he had to after his wreck. He only got a few bruises, but his car was totaled."

"When did all this happen?" I asked.

"The wreck was Friday. He bought the new car on Saturday."

"Terrible things like that happen to good people sometimes," said Honey Lady. "Don't be angry or blame your parents. They couldn't help what happened."

Blame my parents? I hadn't thought about blaming anyone, but I guess it *was* their fault, wasn't it? It made me think—just how much had Dad spent on this new car of his? Had he looked into our account first and figured how much was available before it sent the family into a second financial crisis?

Lauren sat with her eyes closed, one finger rubbing a straight line up and down the middle of her forehead. I pulled her hand down and held on to it. "Was it . . . bad when they came to get you?" *As bad as when they took me?* I meant. Had she been too terrified to think straight? Did Abbie cry and scream as they dragged Lauren away?

"I wouldn't say *bad*," she said. "It was more of a surprise. We weren't out shopping like last time. I would've been much more scared if you hadn't been taken first and I didn't know you'd be here. We still cried, but not as much as before, because we're getting used to it."

You can get used to anything, I guess. Roofing nails shoved under your toenails. Drops of acid plopping onto your skin. Watching your family ripped apart before your eyes.

"So, tell me what you've been doing since you got here," I said.

"I've made two best friends so far. Chloe, on the third floor, and Taylor. I'm not sure where she went."

"How do you know her if she isn't on your floor?" I asked.

"She came in at the same time I did. We rode in the limousine together. I went over to her room and we had dinner and talked until that lady"—Lauren pointed to Crab Woman at the reception desk—"came in and told us to go to our own rooms and go to sleep. Then in the morning, right when I was barely starting the test, I heard Taylor crying way loud. I peeked out of my door and saw . . ." Lauren's eyes shifted to Honey Lady and then back to me. "I saw her being walked away from her testing room. Miss Smoot, where did Taylor go?"

"Taylor is a First Floor and has been assigned to a work project appropriate for her skill set," said Honey Lady. "Some children don't have even the basic computer skills needed to be productive in the workhouse. We can't accommodate children with limited intellectual abilities." A nice way of saying they don't want any stupid kids here. "After they're tested, First Floors remain in

150 this facility only for the short time they spend waiting to

be transported to their permanent assignment in a labor-oriented workhouse. A van comes by once a week to pick up any First Floors we've accumulated."

My stomach sank. Those child slave-labor workhouses I dreaded when I first came here really might exist.

I was almost afraid to ask. "What kind of work do they do?"

"Oh, those workhouses are wonderful!" The cheerleader was back in full force. "Sometimes it's the best thing that can happen for these kids. They acquire real skills as they work on projects such as carpentry, baking, or agriculture—skills that can transfer into jobs in these trades as the kids transition into adulthood. When they go to the labor workhouses, it's almost like they're getting an apprenticeship."

Yeah, I remember reading about apprenticeships in history books too. Some of the apprentices were treated worse than the poor kids in the old workhouses.

"I still don't understand why you're here, Lauren. I mean, we were already over the limit. That's what made them take me."

She just shrugged and shook her head. Her middle finger went back to rubbing.

"Hon . . . Miss Smoot, do you know?"

"I'd have to look up that information." She shook

out her hair and lifted her chin. "Why don't you two discuss your school schedules? Talk about which subjects you each enjoy."

I turned slowly to face her. *Thanks for your opinion, but why do you care what we talk about?* Why was she sitting so close to us anyway?

"Can Lauren and I take a walk outside?" I asked, standing up.

Honey Lady smiled, and her voice was all happy and sweet, even though her words weren't. "No. I'm sorry. You'd have to complete the required paperwork first."

Was she kidding? "We just want a little fresh air. Aren't grown-ups supposed to encourage kids to do that?"

"Matt, I thought you understood by now. A limited amount of adult supervisors are responsible for a large number of children in this facility. Many layers of precautionary measures exist to ensure the safety of every last resident here."

"Fine." I slumped back down on the sofa, folding my arms across my chest. Lauren sat slumped even more than I was, with her head flopped back on the sofa. Her eyes were squeezed tight as if she were tired or . . . oh, no—in pain. Another headache. She hadn't been here very long. She shouldn't be getting them already.

"You could discuss your favorite ways to spend your free hours," said Honey Lady.

"We talk. A lot," said Lauren, without moving or opening her eyes. "Live and in person. We can't text. No bars."

I watched her closely, trying to assess how bad she was feeling. "That must drive you insane."

"Yes! And my friends back home aren't very good with anything other than their stupid phones." Her head popped up and her eyes were on fire. "I e-mailed Shayla today and told her if she doesn't write me back right *now*, I'm never going to talk to her again, and we will *not* buy matching earrings to wear on the field trip to the state capital—if I'm home in time." The eyes closed and the head flopped back again.

"Hang on, are you having trouble receiving e-mails from the outside too?"

Honey Lady jumped to her feet. "I'm sorry, but I could only get you two a few minutes of visitation today. It has now expired, and I'm going to have to escort you back to your floors."

Lauren moaned softly.

"Are you okay?" I asked her.

"Right now," said Honey Lady.

"Wait. Something's the matter with her."

"I'm all right," said Lauren, wincing as she pushed herself off the sofa.

"She's just tired." Honey Lady nudged us forward.   153

"It takes a while to get used to a new schedule and routine. Plus, I bet I'm correct in assuming that you've been doing a lot of talking with your friends after lights-out, haven't you?"

With a sheepish shrug, Lauren nodded.

"Come along." Honey Lady was laying on the sugar pretty thick again. "I'll try to arrange another visit for you two soon. All right? You say you want an out-of-doors visit next time? That will take longer to get clearance, but I'll get right on it."

"The rules around here stink," said Lauren.

"You're right about that."

"I'm terribly sorry. I wish there were more I could do." Honey Lady held out her arm, as if showing us the way to the elevator. *Gee, thanks. We'd forgotten where it was.* The blond guard appeared in the hallway behind Crab Woman's desk. He didn't have to flex his muscles in our faces. We weren't going to rebel or break out—at least not yet.

Honey Lady stayed on our heels as Lauren and I walked to the elevator.

"I don't think we'll get lost," I said.

"It's all right," said Honey Lady. "I don't mind riding along. I need to speak with a few Third Floors anyway."

The elevator doors closed the three of us inside, and
we stood staring at the line down the middle of them.

With her hands at her waist, Honey Lady's long fingernails tapped at a machine-gun pace against the hard case of the cell phone attached to her front pocket. "Go ahead and say your name, Lauren." The gulping gasp of air Honey Lady sucked in made me turn around.

"Lauren!" I yelled. "What's wrong with her?"

My little sister's eyelids fluttered, and all I could see was the whites of her eyeballs. She kept sucking in quick, shallow breaths, but she never seemed to let any of them out.

"Lauren!" I grabbed on to her arms and felt the muscles underneath the skin twitching like crazy. I scowled at Honey Lady. "Why are you just standing there? Do something!"

"Just wait." She pulled out a pocket computer, checked her watch, and typed in some info.

"Lauren." I gave her a little shake. "Can you hear me?"

The eyes slowed down and closed. Her entire body sagged against me, like a scarecrow off his pole.

"See? I knew she'd be fine. Sharlene Smoot, third floor."

CHAPTER 16

"ARE YOU SICK, MATT? YOU DON'T look too good."

I didn't feel too good.

Jeffery set the circuit board and miniature light bulbs he was carrying onto the floor outside the rec room and reached out to steady me. "Do you need help?"

Without answering, I continued to zombie-walk away from him and toward my room. I went inside, leaving the door open, and headed straight for the bed. As stiff and straight as a line segment, I fell forward onto my face.

"Bro? You okay?"

"He looked really white and sort of wobbled as he walked," I heard Jeffery's voice say.

"It's okay, dude, you were right to get me." Coop's hand shook my shoulder. "Roll over, man. You gotta breathe."

Remaining on my stomach, I turned my head enough to let air reach my nostrils.

"Are you going to get better in time for water jousting tonight?" asked Jeffery. "I finished making the paddles."

"He's one sick dude."

"I'll call Miss Smoot."

"No!" I sprang to my knees, then twisted around to face them. "She . . . thinks Lauren's fine." My voice went whiny. *"Just a little stress."* I punched the mattress next to my leg. "She dragged her onto the third floor and shoved me back inside the elevator."

"Whoa, bro, you hit your head or something?" He lifted up one of my eyelids. "You okay in there?"

I shoved his arm away.

"My sister, Lauren. Remember I told you about her being here—that I was going to see her today? She had some sort of fit in the elevator. She blacked out for a minute and went all shaky and freaky."

"Psycho!" Coop wiggled his fingers in front of my face.

"It's not funny! Something's wrong, and Honey Lady isn't even going to call my parents."

"Hold up, bro. Honey who?"

Major foot in mouth. I was too upset to care much, though.

"Nothing. Never mind. I asked Miss Smoot to call my parents, and she said they don't need to worry." 157

Turning, I punched the headboard this time. Pain crunched my knuckles, but I barely noticed. "My parents need to know!"

Jeffery plopped down on the end of my bed. "*You* can tell them. Send them an e-mail."

"A lot of good that will do."

The two of them stared at me, blankly.

"My e-mails never get through. Miss Smoot claims there's a *technical problem* with my account, but the more I think about it, the more I think she's lying. Doesn't it seem weird to you? No cell phone service. The landline phones are only for in-house use. I don't know why I'm different, but my e-mails to the outside never get answered. How do they expect us to talk to our parents?"

"My 'rents e-mail me back all the time," said Coop. "But you're right, they never get around to answering my questions. They just give me boring play-by-plays of their boring lives. I think I'm an item on their to-do lists now. They never joke or get off on weird tangents like the way they used to talk. It's no fun commun'ing with them anymore."

Jeffery's mouth got tight. "My parents would never answer my e-mail—even if I sent them any."

"Well, I know my e-mails aren't getting through, and I'm pretty sure Lauren's aren't either." Shaking my head, I slid off the side of the bed. "I gotta get out of here.

Either of you guys ever go outside?" If I could get to the grounds without a gorilla guard breathing down my neck, I might just be able to make a break for it.

"I tried once." Jeffery pushed his glasses up his nose as he looked at me. "I had to fill out a bunch of forms and give my reasons and explain in detail what I was going to do out there. I just wanted to try a model airplane I'd ordered. It took ten days before permission came, and that day turned out to be windy and cold."

I did a loop around the sofa, snatching a pillow off it and punching it as I paced. "There has to be a way. Guys, you've gotta help me. My parents have to know about Lauren, and the only way it's going to happen is if I go home and tell them."

The answer came fast. The details of how to carry it out came more slowly.

All we had to do was deactivate the security monitors for a while and sneak me past Crab Woman at the reception desk. No prob.

While one side of my brain concentrated on the computer and hacking my way into the workhouse's security network, the three of us tossed around ideas about how to get through the first floor without being seen. Since shooting Crab Woman and the gorilla guards with a tranquilizer dart wasn't a viable option, we seriously considered my trying a desperate dash through the lobby, knocking over anyone who got in my way.

"I don't know," I said. "I don't think I can football-tackle any of those guards. Come on, guys. I'm almost in. Think fast. Any minute now they might decide to take a hard look at their link to my computer. They'll realize I'm not just surfing the Net and shut me down."

"That's amazing," said Jeffery. "How are you doing that so fast?"

I shrugged one shoulder. "I've hacked into a different section of their system before. Come on, guys. I've gotta go tonight."

Coop shoved the last of the taquitos we'd ordered into his mouth and didn't bother to wait until he swallowed before he talked. "No sweat, bro. I've got it all worked out. You gotta turn invisible, dude."

"Right." Chuckling, I shook my head. "Great idea. You go ahead and make that happen." I worked a few more minutes. "Got it!" I jumped up, knocking the chair back hard as I threw my arms high in the air. "Yes! I just made every last security screen go black. It's not going to last long. I've gotta make a break for it right now. It's dark outside. If I can just make it through the door, I have a good shot at getting away before they see me. Maybe the guards will be too busy with the screens to notice me sneaking out. I bet I can outrun Crab Woman."

"The receptionist?" Jeffery slapped his thigh. "Good one. And Honey Lady is Miss Smoot! I get it now. Do you have one for anyone else? How about me?"

"Uh, no." I headed for the door.

"Hold up, dude. You're not making some crazy sprint. I told you. Invisibility. Come on, Jeffery boy. We've got a buddy to make disappear."

The beeps from the top-floor smoke detector lasted a few seconds longer this time, because Coop made extra smoke by relighting the paper each time it went out. The sound of the three of us pounding down the stairs echoed up and around the tall, narrow stairwell. My ears needed a break. They'd get one soon. A few more steps and I'd be on the first floor. *Please let the security cameras still be out.*

Coop pushed past me. "We're going first, bro."

What? No way. He was going to blow my cover! I grabbed at him, but he slipped through the door to the first floor too fast.

"What are you doing?" I was banking big-time on the element of surprise helping me slip past Crab Woman. Coop and Jeffery made more noise than Madeline at her peak. I clutched my hair, wanting to scream. Coop didn't even try to sneak. He walked into the middle of the lobby, pulling a confused Jeffery behind him. I inched to the end of the hall, flat and out of sight against the wall.

"Hey, what's happening?" Coop said, with a goofy wave to Crab Woman.

"How did you get down here? Return to your floor at once," she said, the gravel thick in her voice.

"No prob. We're just going outside for a little walk first. We'll be right back. On my honor." With a laugh, he traced a sloppy X over his heart.

Crab Woman jumped to her feet. "Young man!" She pointed at Jeffery. "You. Take your friend upstairs."

"I'm sorry, ma'am," said Jeffery, crinkling his nose under his glasses. "It's a perfect night for stargazing, and I've just got to teach my friend here how to spot the Big Dipper."

"Yeah, right." Coop burst out laughing, slapping him on the arm. "You can be funny when you want, little bro. Let's go."

With that Coop turned and sprinted toward the door. Unlike automatic shopping-center doors, this one didn't slide open as he approached.

"Aw, man," said Coop, banging his fist against the glass.

Crab Woman groaned as she trudged around the side of her desk and across the lobby.

"You coming to let us out?" Coop bounced back toward Crab Woman.

"I most certainly am not!"

"That's cool. We'll just try the back door." With that

he zipped around a large armchair and made a break for the hallway that stretched behind Crab Woman's desk.

She pointed at him, her mouth dropping in surprise. "Stop!"

Jeffery, wearing an innocent smile, shrugged at Crab Woman and took off after Coop.

"Security!" Crab Woman didn't quite run after the guys, but she moved in a faster scuffle. "Where are they? They've never let things go this far before. I have half a mind to unlock the back door and let those monsters leave."

I know I'm really smart, but sometimes I surprise myself at how stupid I can be. Crab Woman had vanished from my line of sight down the hall before I figured out what Coop and Jeffery were doing. They were creating a distraction. By drawing one hundred percent of Crab Woman's attention toward themselves, they made me invisible.

Not waiting another second, I sprinted into the lobby and headed for Crab Woman's desk, hoping to find a button sitting in the middle of it clearly labeled PRESS HERE TO OPEN FRONT DOORS. No luck.

I yanked at the top drawer. *Please, please, please.* It was locked. Seconds were ticking away fast, and I knew I hadn't started with many in the first place. I felt underneath the desk, to see if a button was hidden there. The only thing I felt was smooth wood.

A soft thump down one of the hallways behind me made my heart rate skyrocket. I had to get out of the lobby—out of the building—now! I ran to the door, hoping that by some miracle it would open for me. It didn't. I dug my fingers into the crack in the middle, trying to jimmy it apart.

"Hey!"

My shoulders jerked up to my ears. I froze. I'd been caught. It was over.

"What do you think you're doing, kid?" a gorilla guard bellowed. It was the one who wore a goatee.

I couldn't say anything.

He lumbered around the reception desk and wove through the sofa and chairs toward me. For a minute all I could do was stand there and stare at him. When he got within five feet, I reacted like a jackrabbit facing a salivating wolf. I ran.

I didn't have a plan or a destination and ended up sprinting down the nearest hallway—the one where my first-night room and testing room were located. I don't know where I thought I'd be able to hide in there. It was dark. That could help.

The one good thing about the guard's bulky muscles was they slowed him down. I'd cream him in a footrace any day, if I had somewhere to run.

I shoved doors open on my left and on my right. If he

stopped to look inside each room, I'd gain an even bigger lead on him—a lead to a dead end. *Whoopee.*

The darkness at the end of the hall closed in around me. I felt, more than saw, the last door on the left side and slipped through, closing it silently behind me. With my hands stretched out, feeling the air like a mime, I moved deep inside the room, trying to lose myself in the dark space. I didn't get far. The room ended up being a ten-by-three-foot housecleaning closet, by the feel of the bottles and buckets on the shelves. My fingers followed the shelves along the left-hand side of the room. They made a sharp turn and ran the length of the back wall.

A loud clunk made me freeze. The guard had made it about halfway down the hall, by the sound of it. A thin line of light appeared near the floor, under the door. Genius Goatee Gorilla Twin had realized that he'd have a better chance of finding me if he turned on the lights. It wouldn't take long now.

I had to hide somewhere fast. Problem was, there just wasn't anyplace to go. He was too close for me to try to get to a different room, and the shelves in here were too short for me to try to climb between. The shelves against the back wall ended at the right wall. It was smooth. No big broom cabinet for me to slip inside. I felt farther. My fingers rose over a thick vertical bump. I held my breath as I frantically investigated by touch and found a waist-high horizontal bar. A door. If luck was on my side, it would be an emergency exit—and not one linked to a smoke detector.

Holding my breath, I pushed through the door. A gust of cool air hit me in the face. I breathed in deep. Fresh, nonfiltered, outside air. *Ahhh.* Before I could take my second breath, a loud clanging alarm blew apart the silent space. The guard would have no problem tracking my location now. It didn't matter. The footrace was on.

The next thing I knew, giant floodlights lit up the grounds. I paused for a second, squinting in the overwhelming brightness. Then I ran, heading across the grass toward the trees.

"Get back here!" The voice sounded deep and angry and full of muscle. I imagined the guard tearing up the ground between us, jumping me from behind, and ripping me to pieces. I pushed harder.

I eyed the flat road stretching in front of the workhouse. The smooth surface would be less hazardous to run on than the obstacle course of the wooded area along the side, but running on the road seemed like a great way to get spotted and caught. I kept to the trees. Running. Always running.

Thanks, Coop, for keeping me in shape.

I MADE IT TO A MORE CROWDED section of the city by morning. Had I only been walking for one night? It felt like a week. I could've lain down on the road and not even twitched if a semi truck zoomed by an inch away from my head. My grouchy, empty stomach made life miserable on a different level.

"Hand over your parental permission card," Corn Dog Pushcart Man said, after I approached him.

Shoot. I hadn't thought about my card for weeks. I couldn't even remember where I'd put it in my room at the workhouse.

"I'm on a special program," I said to the man. "Will you try the scan without the card? Please? I'm starving."

I got my corn dog. Whatever accounting system the FDRA had me on at the workhouse apparently worked out in the real world too.

After squirting a giant glob of mustard on top, I sank in my teeth. Mmm. Heaven on a stick. I enjoyed every bite, even though I knew it came at a high price. The instant Corn Dog Man took the eye scan, my identity and location were broadcast to anyone who cared to look for me, and I didn't wonder for a single second whether or not the FDRA people were looking for me.

What was I thinking? Actually, I hadn't thought very far beyond breaking out of the workhouse. I hadn't even thought to bring my cell phone with me. If I'd been able to charge it back up, I'm sure it would have worked just fine out here. Where did I think I could go without the FDRA finding me? They had to know I'd head for home. Okay. Focus. My goal had been to tell my parents that Lauren was sick. It might also be good to ask them what was going on with our limit that landed her in the workhouse in the first place. All I needed to do was dodge the FDRA people long enough to talk to my parents. First priority, get as far away from Corn Dog Man as fast as possible.

Eye scans work for me out here. I flagged down a taxi.

I slept most of the way home and had the driver drop me off a couple blocks away from my house. I jumped fences and ran through yards, staying out of sight in the shrubbery as much as possible. The closer I got to home, the tighter my stomach knotted up. Since the probability was high that a big black limo was sitting in front of my house at that very moment, I sneaked in through the back door.

Once inside, I paused to catch my breath. Voices and music from the TV in the family room echoed through the otherwise silent house. I walked carefully, trying not to make any noise as I slipped into the family room to see who was watching the set. I don't know why I felt I needed to sneak. This was my house. I had a right to be here.

I found Abbie on the floor on her stomach, mesmerized by people in weird costumes dancing across the TV screen.

"Hey, Abs." I spoke softly, not wanting to startle her.

"Matt!" She jumped to her feet, ran over, and threw her arms around me. "You're home. Did you bring Lauren? Why did you go away for so long?"

Now wasn't the time to explain it all. "Where's Mom?"

"Um . . . I dunno," she said.

"That's okay. I'll find her."

Instead of lying back down in front of the TV, Abbie hooked a finger through one of the belt loops on the back of my pants and followed me closer than a shadow.

We wandered through the kitchen, the dining room, the front room. No Mom. We tried upstairs next. That's where I found her. She sat propped against a pile of pillows on her bed, her bare feet bopping to the music pumping into her brain through her earbuds. Her laptop sat on her thighs, and the sound of her fingers tapping was like a cloudburst against a windowpane.

"Hi, Mom," I said.

She sat up straight, pulled out her earbuds, and pushed the computer off her lap. "Matt!" She jumped off the bed and ran over to me, hugging me tight. "Miss Smoot called from the workhouse, telling me you might show up here. And someone came to the door, looking for you. In fact, he may still be . . . oh, never mind about that. I want to hear from *you* what's going on. I hope you haven't gotten yourself into any serious trouble. How did you get here? Let me look at you." She pushed me out to arm's length for two seconds, then pulled me in for more hugging. "I swear, you've grown taller in the three weeks you've been gone. They must be feeding you well at the workhouse."

"I eat great there," I said. "They can't match your meat loaf, though."

She loosened her hold on me and ruffled my hair. "I'll make some for dinner. Will you get to stay that long?"

"Mom, listen, don't worry about dinner. It's Lauren. Something is wrong with her. Yesterday she had some sort of fit, and they're not going to do anything about it.

She needs to see a doctor or go to the hospital or something."

"It's called a seizure, and she had an extremely mild one, from what Miss Smoot told me. I know they can be frightening. It must have been hard for you to watch."

It was as if I'd smashed into a brick wall, killing my momentum. That word. Seizure. Some kid had one on the first night I was at the workhouse. I didn't know a whole lot about seizures, but I *knew* they weren't anywhere near as common as headaches. And Mom already knew Lauren had one. "Miss Smoot . . . told you?"

"Yes. I told you she called me a little while ago."

Right. When Honey Lady realized they weren't going to catch me before I made it home, she figured she'd better cover her tracks.

"It's so sweet of you to be worried about your sister. But that's my job. And your father's—and believe me, we've done plenty. Miss Smoot sent us an electronic copy of Lauren's medical records and assured us that the workhouse has medical personnel on-site. No children there are going to go without the medical attention they need. Lauren was thoroughly examined. We made sure of that. She's fine. It was just a fluke."

"A fluke? Mom, she's been at the workhouse for what—six days? She's never had a seizure before in her life. Do you really think that's a coincidence?"

"What are you saying? You can't think something at the workhouse caused the seizure. That's ridiculous."

"Why? At least one other kid I know of has had a seizure since I've been there."

"I can't worry about all the other kids in the work-house. I'm just concerned with my two."

"Well, what about all the headaches?"

Mom rubbed the side of her forehead. "I think I'm developing one right now."

"Aren't you going to do something?"

"About what?"

"Getting Lauren out of there!"

Shaking her head, she plopped down on the bed. "Oh, Matt. Don't you think that's what I'm trying to do? It's what we've all been trying to do—ever since the moment they took you."

I sat down next to her, reaching for the laptop. "Okay. Show me what you've been doing."

"Show you?" Her eyebrows crinkled together. "How? It's not like I've been drawing up pie charts and graphs."

"Just show me the numbers in our account. I'm sure it's all online somewhere."

As I forced the computer on her, her fingertips balanced it on the edge of her lap. "Yes. I'm sure it is all on here somewhere."

"Don't you check it regularly? Mom! How can you

know how far over the limit we are if you don't check the account? Did you ever check it before we went over?"

Mom looked like she'd just been stung by a bee. "I don't like to worry about money. Dad always assures me we have plenty coming in and that he'll take care of everything."

"Great. That's just great." My breath came out in a big gushing sigh. "Mom, managing the account isn't calculus. Heck, it isn't even algebra. Basic, simple arithmetic."

"Oh, no. It's much more complicated than that. It's got all that interest to calculate and the fines and fees to figure out."

"Okay, but *you* don't have to figure out that part. The software does it for you. All you have to do is take a look. Addition and subtraction are the only things you need to figure out how much over or under the limit we are."

Abbie bounced on the bed behind us. With a loud, giggly squeal she launched herself at my back, wrapping her arms in a stranglehold around my neck.

"Knock it off," I said, untangling myself. Turning, I saw her lips pout out and her eyes fill with tears. "I'll play with you in a few minutes. Okay? After I'm done talking to Mom. Here, give me that." I reclaimed the computer and within a few seconds found the site that would connect us to our family account. Mom placed her thumb on the scanner pad, but she couldn't remember the password. I had to wait for several minutes while she answered a long list of security questions.

"All right," I said, taking over the computer once again. "Let's see what's going on. What I don't get is why Lauren got taken away. How could we go over the limit when we were already over the limit?"

"Oh. That."

"Tell me."

She didn't have to say a word. I could see it for myself. Two lines of account activity were listed for the very same date.

MATTHEW DUNSTON BROUGHT IN TO SATISFY FDO 169-D.

And then,

DUNSTON FAMILY LIMIT INCREASE ACTIVATED.

Our limit had gone up because of my work at the FDRA. *Glad to be of service, Mom and Dad. Anything else you want from me? A quart of blood maybe? A kidney?*

"You knew about this all along?"

Squeezing her lips together, she nodded. "We received a phone call soon after you left."

"Why didn't they send me home as soon as you got the new limit?"

"They couldn't." Mom reached for a tissue. "If you

came home, we would drop back down to the old limit. *That's* the one we have to get under in order for you to be able to come home."

"And you didn't even make an effort." My voice grew louder as the picture of what had been going on around here came more clearly into focus. I started breathing fast, like I'd just come off a three-mile race. "You went over the new limit too. That's what made them take Lauren. How could you do that to her?"

She blew into her tissue. "We *have* been making an effort. That's what I don't understand. The in-home care we had to get for Nana isn't cheap, but we thought we had plenty to cover it. Even with the new car, we should have been fine. I didn't even go to the store that day. I hardly bought anything online. Your father went to court to pay the fine for his accident—which really wasn't his fault, so he shouldn't have had to pay it in the first place. It was a good chunk of money, but we still should have been under the limit. And then I got the call that we'd gone over. We couldn't think of a single thing we could do about it."

So you sold off another child.

"You know what, Mom? I can think of a couple of things you could have done. How about stop spending money?" My voice was near screaming now. Blood pounded fast through my head. "Just. Don't. Buy. Anything!" My chest

175

rose and fell in quick succession. "Turn this thing off, and don't open it until both Lauren and I come home!" I slammed the laptop closed and hurled it across the room. It smashed against a wall and fell to the floor.

"Matt!" Mom's voice burst out in surprise and shock.

I snatched up one of Dad's heavy dress shoes off the floor by the bed, stood up, and chucked it at the computer with a roaring scream. The shoe hit the wall and left a black mark on the cream wallpaper. Maybe the mate would hit the computer.

"Stop it!" Mom stood next to me, her hands tugging my arm. She wasn't strong enough to hold me back, and the second shoe went even farther off target, smashing into an assortment of perfume bottles on a small vanity table. The mix of strong flowery and spicy aromas stung my nose. I searched the floor for another pair of shoes, even though I knew that breaking stuff was stupid. My parents would just run out and buy a new laptop and restock the perfume bottles. *Go ahead, Mom and Dad. Rack up the account. Don't worry about the limit. You've got one more kid left to sell off.*

Abbie's soft whimpers finally got through to me. I dropped the shoe I'd grabbed from the closet and turned to her. She huddled in a tight ball behind a couple of the pillows on the bed, the tips of her fingers in her mouth.

"It's okay, Abbie," I said. "I'm sorry."

"You should be," said Mom.

Abbie didn't budge.

"What were you thinking?" Mom asked. "You show up out of the blue and start destroying things, scaring your little sister to death. It's inexcusable."

Inexcusable? Me?

"Just blatant disrespect for family members," I snapped back. "A behavioral technique I learned from you."

"That's not fair, Matt, and I will not have you talk to me like that in my own home!"

"You know what to do, then, don't you? Keep spending money. Then you'll never have to worry about me saying another word in this house ever again."

She paused, pained lines creasing her forehead between her eyes. Didn't stop me.

"How dare you, Mom? You do realize you only have Abbie left now. What are you going to do when they come for her and you're out of kids?"

The trembling fingers of Mom's hand rose to her mouth as she lowered herself to sit on the edge of her bed.

Abbie started crying big-time. Shoot. I shouldn't have said anything about her getting taken away. She'd already seen Lauren and me go. She had to be scared about the big black limo coming for her someday.

Mom held out her hand and Abbie crawled into her hug.

177

"Don't worry, sweetie, no one will take you away." Mom glanced up at me. "She's too young. They won't take her."

"How do you know? Have you checked it out already?" My voice sounded so mean I didn't recognize it. I threw my arms out to my sides. "Don't you and Dad care that we're gone?"

Mom squeezed her eyes closed and gave her head a shake, as if clearing something out of it. "You have no idea how much I care, Matt. Dad, too. It's killing us to have you and Lauren gone. We're both working extremely hard to get the two of you home."

"Right," I said, rolling my eyes.

"No! It's true. That's what I was working on when you came in. I'm starting a new business! As soon as it takes off, we'll get the two of you home right away."

The adrenaline pulsing through me slacked off a tiny bit. "Really?"

"Yes, I have two appointments this very afternoon, and your father has one this evening."

Any extra money Mom and Dad brought in would totally benefit our account. They were both taking on an extra job, just to get us under the limit—to get me home. "What's the business?"

"Marketing," she said, her voice taking on an excited bounce. "There's this incredibly fast-growing company that makes amazing health products—energy boosters, antioxidant supplements, things like that. The amazing part is that the supplements come in these little, matchstick-sized rods that are inserted under the skin of the upper arm. A tiny computer chip analyzes the body's needs and releases the supplements automatically. Isn't that fantastic? I'm telling you, Matt, these products will practically sell themselves. And what's even better, if Dad and I recruit other people to join our sales force, we get a commission for every product they sell. Then, when they recruit more people, we get a percentage of their commissions as well, and it goes on and on. Soon we won't have to worry about doing any selling of our own. We can just sit back and count the money rolling in from the sellers underneath us."

The smile on my face flattened out. "I don't understand how that can work."

"It's simple, sweetie. They ask each new salesperson—or team, in our case—to recruit ten new people. If each of them recruits ten people, we'll earn a commission from one hundred and ten people. Imagine all that money. Imagine how much we'll earn when those one hundred people recruit ten people each, and then those people recruit ten people each."

"Stop," I said, holding out my hands. "It's impossible, Mom. It sounds like a total scam."

"No, it's not a scam. I have a long list of people and their testimonials of how they made piles of money working with this company."

"If that were true, then it would be even more impossible for you to make anything. You've got to look at this mathematically. If what you're saying is true, the sales force would grow at an exponential rate. It wouldn't take long before the world would run out of people to recruit. Besides that, with all these people selling, who's buying?"

"A lot of people want these products," said Mom, sticking her chin in the air. "They practically sell themselves."

"How many have you sold?" I asked.

She hesitated. "Well, none yet. We've been focusing our time on recruiting. That's where the real money will come from. We'll start selling after we have our ten people. We could get our first three recruits today, after our appointments. When we're ready to sell, we've got a whole closet full of products waiting to ship out. You'll see, Matt. It will work. It *has* to work."

Closing my eyes, I tilted my head back. "Please tell me the company didn't make you pay for those products before they sent them to you." It was as if I could see dollar signs flying out the window in front of me. "Don't tell me you had to put up a bunch of money to get into this." I already knew they had. How else could that stupid company earn any money when their entire sales force was focusing on finding more sellers instead of pushing product?

"You know what your father always says: 'You've got to spend money to make money.' This business is guaranteed to turn a profit in mere weeks. It's sure to tide us over until your father lands some new clients."

My heart skipped a beat. "What's the matter with his old ones?"

"He finished all the projects he had contracted to do. Right now he's focused on acquiring new projects."

"What about that Dupree project?" I asked.

"It never worked out. Your father is hopeful about several new leads he has. I'm sure he'll secure something soon. If not, maybe this new marketing venture will turn into his full-time job as well."

The dollars in our account disappeared faster than I could think of them. I sank down on the bed, my head drooping into my hands.

"Matt." Along with her soothing words, Mom stroked her fingers through my hair. "I know you're frustrated that it's going to take a while before you can come home, but it's not as if you're being hurt in the meantime. Miss Smoot e-mails me regularly about how well you and Lauren are doing. You've both made lots of new friends. You're doing exceptionally well in your schoolwork, and just look at the job experience you're getting. Think what an amazing resume you'll be able to put together once you get out. Miss Smoot also sent me pictures of the workhouse." Mom gave me a playful jab on the leg. "Talk about cushy. Don't you just love it there? I worry that you won't want to come home when the time comes."

I took a long, hard look at her, and a big lump tightened in my chest. *Would* I want to come home when I was able? I'd always assumed I would, but now that I thought about it, I had to wonder—especially after this. Living on the top floor was pretty cool, but home was *home*. Either way, if my parents kept managing our family account with this crazy logic, I doubted I'd ever get to make that choice.

CHAPTER 18

I WASN'T SURPRISED TO SEE THE
FDRA limo outside with Gorilla Man
leaning against the trunk. What *had* surprised me was the fact that Mom had
totally bought into the whole the-FDRA-workhouse-is-
a-fabulous-place, don't-worry-that-it's-making-your-
kids-have-convulsions bit. I didn't care what Honey
Lady said or how convinced Mom was. Seizures were a
big deal. If nobody else was going to help Lauren, I'd
have to do it myself.

Mom hadn't said a whole lot more, and Abbie—still
freaked by my shoe-throwing tantrum—stuck close to
Mom on the bed and slurped her thumb like it was a
root-beer Popsicle.

No matter what I said, Mom was convinced her
new "business venture" was going to bring in piles
of money. What was the minimum age for kids at
the workhouse? I hadn't seen any kids younger than
about eleven. So unless the FDRA changed the rules
again, that gave us five years before Abbie showed up.

I'd be eighteen by then—legally the government would have to set me free and give me an individual limit—but Lauren would still be there. The chances of my entire family ever living at home together again were about as good as the product of two positive numbers coming out negative.

The front door slammed behind me as I stepped onto my front porch. Gorilla Man popped to his feet, turning to look at me. His face wrinkled with confusion. He looked back down the road—where he'd been keeping watch for my arrival—and then at me again.

"I'm ready," I said, holding up my hands to show I wasn't going to put up a fight. "Let's go."

I stared at the black privacy glass during the entire two-hour drive, thinking what it would be like to spend almost my entire teenage life at the workhouse. No attending Friday night high school football games. No being the star of the school math team and chess club. No prom—I like to think I'd have been cool enough by senior year to get a girlfriend.

"You, young man!" Crab Woman's always grainy voice welcomed me back. "You've caused a lot of bother for us around here. Don't think you've gotten away with anything. Miss Smoot will be coming up to the top floor just as soon as she can break away from a meeting. Do you hear me?"

I waved limply at her as I moved toward the elevator, still lost in my own thoughts. Gorilla Man followed closely, but he didn't go upstairs with me.

I realized something else I'd miss in here—my driver's license!

"Hey, bro, you're back. What gives? They catch you?" Coop's voice barely registered in my brain.

I walked into my room, thinking only, *I'm here forever*. Mom and Dad were living it up on the outside, thanks to the new limit I'd given them. Why should they have all the fun? Maybe I wanted to buy some things too.

I sat down at the computer and started clicking. Why not? Neither of my parents cared about the limit or how high our debt racked up. I'd show them I didn't care either.

I bought everything. Dozens of transactions. I didn't even know what I was buying. I just pointed and clicked. Designer handbag. Sure, that looked good. Point, click, eye scan. Top-of-the-line espresso machine. The scent of coffee made me queasy, but who cared? Point, click, eye scan. A jackhammer. Ruby earrings. A dog kennel. I bought it all.

Man, the boxes were sure going to pile up outside my door over the next few days.

Hey. Wait a minute. Boxes.

The computer chair made a popping noise as I sprang out of it.

"Jeffery?" I called down the hall, even though I had no idea if he was anywhere near his bedroom. I passed Coop's door and banged on the next one, taking note of the pile of freshly delivered boxes on the floor. "Jeffery, you in there?"

A minute later he opened it. "Oh, it's you! Are we ready for water jousting now? I'll grab the paddles. . . ."

"Hang on." I slapped my palm against his door to keep it from closing on me. Easing it back open wide, I took a couple of steps inside. "Here. I'll help you." Man, oh man. I had to stop and check my bearings for a minute. Jeffery's room had the exact same floor plan and furniture as mine, but that was the end of the similarities. A LEGO skyscraper as thick as a cinder block stood in one corner, reaching all the way to the tall ceiling. Smaller LEGO buildings were in the construction phase around it. Swords and other medieval weapons covered an entire wall, each with a gold identification plate above it like it was in a museum. The name of one sword, King Arthur's Excalibur, I recognized. These were no cheap plastic or aluminum models. These were heavy-duty, intricately detailed, probably-sharp-enough-to-slice-your-thumb-off duplicates. An aquarium that had to be five feet long stretched against the wall by his bed, filled with exotic-looking fish. But that wasn't everything. There were also the boxes—

piles, stacks, mounds of them everywhere. Most of them unopened.

I tapped the tip of my shoe lightly against a nearby box. "Looks like you've been ordering a lot of stuff since you got here."

Jeffery popped up on the far side of his bed, holding up two long kayak paddles. Each of the ends had been padded with a three-foot diameter foam ball and then covered in heavy-duty vinyl. One was black. One was blue.

"Cool, huh? See, we can pound each other with these and never get hurt."

"Jeffery, you're a smart kid."

"I know. You like them?"

"Yeah, but that's not what I'm getting at. You're a Top Floor. You're a genius in . . . whatever that electronic-simulations stuff is that you do for your job. I'm just . . . lost when it comes to all this." I lifted my arms out wide, gesturing to the mountains of stuff.

Deep lines appeared on his forehead. "What do you mean?"

"You know—I *know* you know—that if you keep ordering stuff like this, you're never going to make it out of here."

He tossed the paddles down on his bed. Hard. "Yeah? You know what? You *are* right. I *do* know that." 187

Weaving around the boxes, he made his way over to me and stood, puffing up his chest as he faced me. A lot of hot air came out of that little guy. "Who says I want to get out?"

I was so surprised, my brain blipped out, and I had to reboot it to get it thinking again.

"You don't want to go home?" I asked. "Ever?"

"Why would I want to leave a place like this?" Stepping back and spreading his arms out wide, he turned in a slow circle. "Look at the setup we've got, Matt. Work is cool. School is even interesting here. In a few years we'll have moved completely into college-level classes. Once we turn eighteen, we'll be able to write our own tickets in life. We'll get tons of scholarship offers, or even job offers right off the bat. We'll be floating in money." His thumbnail scraped at the packing tape holding a nearby box tightly closed. "If I feel like it, I'll sell off some of this stuff when I get out. Live off the cash for a while, maybe. It *is* getting crowded in here, though. I'm going to have to move away from electronics and go to something smaller, like diamonds. Or gold. Bars of solid gold. The PMC I bought will go a long way toward keeping me here."

"PMC? You mean you bought one of those little personal helicopters?"

"Personal Mini Copter. Yeah. It's so cool. Miss

Smoot won't let me fly it yet—since I can't get a license until I'm sixteen. She lets me store it on the roof, but *she's* keeping the keys locked up somewhere."

I've seen PMCs in action a couple of times. The image of Jeffery flying around in one of those little helicopters brought a smile to my face. If he could buy that now to use later, what was stopping me from ordering a great sports car? Oh, yeah. Reality. "Those PMCs cost almost as much as a car. Don't you care about your family? They'll get stuck with all that debt."

He shrugged. "Serves them right."

"But . . ." I had to stop for a second and admit that I'd been heading down that exact same road not five minutes earlier. "Okay, but don't you miss them? And what about your friends on the outside? Don't you ever want to see them again?"

"Guys like me don't do well in the friend department." He slumped down on an arm of his sofa, hanging his head so I couldn't see his face. "You want to hear about my family?"

I felt my feet taking me a step backward, closer to the door.

His straight black hair hung down over his face. "My dad sits around on his butt all day, watching TV. My mom spends all her waking hours trying to earn money to keep the family going. You'll never believe   189 her brilliant plan to do it. Online slot machines. Now there's a solid career path for anybody, huh?"

He looked up at me for a second and smiled—a weak, miserable smile.

"I have two older brothers. One's in jail, and the other's headed there." Leaning forward with his elbows on his thighs, he clasped his hands together. His knuckles had gone white. "Why would I want to see any of their faces again?"

I found myself backing away another couple of steps.

"I'm just glad my brothers were too messed up to come here, so the FDRA took me. That's the one good thing my brothers did. I have no desire to be in the same room with any of them ever again, and it's cake to make sure I don't have to. My family will never see the underside of their limit again in their lifetimes, and I get to live on the top floor in the meantime." When he tilted his head up to look at me, his lips were trembling all over the place. Small pools of tears had collected at the inner corners of his eyes. "So to answer your question, no. I don't miss my family."

CHAPTER 19

"HELLO, BOYS." THE FEMALE VOICE sent a slice of cold fear into my chest. Jeffery slid an arm across the top half of his face as he did a quick turn to sit on the seat of his sofa, facing the back wall. Girls weren't allowed in the boys' bedrooms. Except one girl. One woman. She sounded too bubbly and syrupy for the lecture I knew she'd come up here to give me. What kind of punishments did they give Top Floors anyway?

I hadn't heard her walk inside the room, so the sensation of her hand slithering onto my shoulder as she came up behind me gave me the creeps more than if someone had dumped a jar of spiders down my arm.

"Quite the collection you've got going here, Jeffery," said Honey Lady.

Not making a sound, he nodded his head.

The shoulder hand slid down to grasp me tight above the elbow. Her long fingernails dug into my skin the tiniest bit. "All right, Matt. Time for our little chat. We'll see you later, Jeffery. Don't buy everything on one website!" She chuckled, as if she'd just made a joke. After closing the door on Jeffery, she forced out another laugh. "And don't you worry, Matt. We're just going to talk. That's it." Her smile was too calm. She seemed too happy as we headed toward my bedroom.

I hitched my thumb back toward Jeffery's room. "Does that bother you at all?"

"Well, of course!"

Good. She *was* a rational person.

She grimaced, completely exposing all of her big, white teeth. "I, personally, would go crazy living among all that clutter."

Maybe not.

"No, I mean, shouldn't you say something to Jeffery?" I tried to pull my arm out of her claws as we walked to my room, but she hung on even tighter. "Is it really right for him to keep buying all that stuff and sabotaging his family's limit?"

"That's something Jeffery is going to have to work out with his family. I have no jurisdiction, and—frankly— it's not my business how other people spend their money. Let's go in." She pointed to my door, waiting for me to open it for her—like I had any choice whether or not I wanted to invite her in.

Doing a quick scan of my room, she noticed my

computer—exactly as I had left it in the middle of ordering a lawn mower.

"You doing a little shopping yourself?" she asked,
lifting one corner of her mouth in a teasing smile.

"No." I reached around her and clicked cancel. "Not
anymore."

"It makes no difference to me." Shrugging, with her
arms out wide, she sauntered over to one of the chairs at
the table. "Order whatever you want."

I sat in the chair across from her. "Maybe later." *Or not.*

"All right, Matt. We've got a problem here."

"I know. I ran off. But I'm back. I *had* to talk to my
mom, and you wouldn't let me."

Her eyebrows bunched together, and she leaned forward, taking one of my hands gently in hers. "What are
you talking about?"

"No cell phone. No e-mail. How do you expect me
to talk to my parents?"

"Guess what? I know for certain that your e-mail
problem is being looked at right this very minute. I
wouldn't be surprised if you were able to communicate
with your parents by tonight!" She beamed at me with so
much enthusiasm I almost expected her to pull out her
cheerleader pom-poms.

I sat back in my chair, pulling my hand away. "That
would be . . . good." I wasn't sure if I bought her story. 193

"It feels like you're cutting us off from our families on purpose."

"That's ridiculous."

"Well, I guess for now it doesn't matter either way. I talked to my mom and found out what I needed to know. I'm back. I'll stay as long as you make me. End of story."

She tilted her head, smiling that sweet smile of hers that had a tendency to turn my brains into sugar crystals. "Oh, Matt. If only it were that simple. I'm afraid you're a security risk now." She dug into the front pocket of her suit jacket and, holding up her index finger, said, "Just one minute." She disappeared, ducking to the side and under the table. Before I could lean over to see what she was doing I felt her hand and something cold and hard around my ankle.

I jerked my leg to the side. "What are you doing?"

"I'm so sorry, Matt." The honey voice stayed just as sugary sweet.

A thick, heavy, metal band was fastened around my ankle. I yanked on it, but it was too tight to slip off and it wouldn't unfasten.

"It's regulation. You're a runner risk now. It's our responsibility to know where every single one of our children is at all times. I'm sure you understand, a smart Top Floor like you."

The rounded edges of the metal band hurt as they dug into my hand, but that didn't make me stop tugging.

"The only way it will unlatch is if I activate a special remote, which is kept locked in a safe in my office. The remote can only be activated by me, after a retina scan."

"There's some sort of tracking device in here?" I banged it against the side of the table.

"Matt. Relax. It's not like you're going to go anywhere anyway. Just pretend it isn't even there. It's not heavy. It's completely waterproof. You can still go swimming!"

Rah! Rah! Matt's on a leash now. Go, fight, win!

My leg froze for a minute, hanging in the air. "It's just for my protection. Right?"

She beamed. "Exactly."

Slowly, my leg sank to the floor. "I can just stay on the top floor and do my work and hang with my buddies and absolutely nothing will happen. It won't send an alarm unless I do something stupid, like try to go down to another floor—which I'll *never* do again, since I know it prevents you from keeping me safe."

She shoved my arm playfully. "You've got it now."

"If I stop trying to take it off, and do exactly what I'm supposed to do, it will come off someday, won't it?"

"We'll see."

"I'll be happy here! I'll work hard and get As on all   195 my school assignments. I'll even order lots of fun things so I'll never want to leave the top floor."

Patting me on the arm, she stood up. "Let's see how things are going in a few weeks. If you can live up to that high standard you just set for yourself, then I don't see any reason why we won't be able to talk about a potential removal date. Okay?"

I smiled what I hoped looked like a sincere, cooperative smile. "Okay."

I sat staring out my window for a long time after she left. Three things I knew for sure now.

(1) Honey Lady didn't care how much stuff we bought. She liked it if we bought enough to keep us distracted from thinking about life on the outside. (2) I was going to have to pretend that I was being a good, compliant little Top Floor until I could figure out exactly what was going on. And (3) When the time was right, ankle monitor or not, I was out of here.

I received my first e-mail from my dad that night, exactly as Honey Lady predicted.

> Hey, buddy,
> Sure miss you. Don't worry about us. We're
> doing great—working hard. We'll have this
> money mess cleared up before you know

it. Leave it all to Mom and me. You just
concentrate on your schoolwork and the job
they're having you do. And don't forget about
having fun! Don't worry about spending money
on things you want or need while you're in
there. Mom and I have everything covered.
See you soon!
Dad

It didn't make me feel connected to him or the out-side world at all. In fact, it made me annoyed. He sounded like he was in league with Honey Lady, encouraging me to spend money. A weird thing for him to say when we were supposed to be watching our account. Was Dad as clueless about money as Mom? If so, then my family was really in trouble.

For four days I played the part of a carefree teen king having a great ol' time living on the top floor, where imagination—and certainly not money—was the only thing holding us back.

Today was the day Jeffery had been dreaming of. He finally talked Coop and me into promising to come out of the gym and into the pool for some jousting. Although we'd been pumped over the idea when we first came up with it, the excitement had worn off for Coop and me, and we'd sort of forgotten about it. That wasn't the case with Jeffery. The minute work was over, he headed straight for the water. I *was* starting to get into the idea again. It could be fun. I was ready to take him on.

Okay, so I wasn't completely ready. I had to change into my swimming trunks, and my floating island still sat folded up in a box. Twenty minutes later, with Coop's help, I finished pumping it.

"For two brilliant top-floor dudes we sure are stupid," said Coop after we tipped the inflated island on its side. It stood four inches taller than my bedroom door. "Way to go, fool."

"Here, hold it up." I jumped and grabbed the top of the island, letting my weight squeeze it down. "Push!"

My body swung forward, and the three of us—me, Coop, and the island—popped through the door. Getting the island out of the hall wasn't a breeze either. How had Jeffery done it? He'd probably been smart enough to inflate his island in the pool room. He kept it there all the time. I'd do the same with this one, once I managed to get it in.

"That puked," Coop said after we bent and squeezed the island into the cubicle room. One of the big, sturdy office chairs we all used blocked our path to the pool room. It was probably Isaac's, but it had gotten pushed out of his cubicle and now sat in front of Reginald's glass box. Coop eyed the chair. "I think I'm due for a nice, long rest."

I laughed. "Yeah, right. As if you could ever hold still for more than ten seconds."

I expected him to keep the joke going by plopping into the chair, spinning around once or twice, and then jumping up and declaring himself rested. I'm sure that's what he intended to do, except he stumbled over something on his way to the chair—his feet, a paper clip, who knew what—and flew forward, his hands straight out to break his fall. His palms hit the backrest, and since the chair was on wheels, the two of them kept right on going, the chair tipping backward as Coop's weight leaned into it.

"Coop!" I stared in shock at the sight of Coop and the chair heading straight for the wall of Reginald's cubicle, and then I clamped my eyes shut and winced as the smooth glass shattered into a thousand pieces. I didn't dare look for several long seconds.

"Augh! I'm dead. I'm bleeding!"

Coop's voice jolted me into action. Leaving the island propped against the wall, I sprang to the cubicle. He'd lucked out big-time. The chair had taken the brunt of the blow, smashing into the glass before any part of Coop's body hit it.

"You're not dead." Roughly shoving the dangling

blinds aside, I pulled him up by one arm, stepping carefully with my bare feet to avoid the sharp chunks of glass lying all around us.

"My eye! I'm bleeding. Bro, I cut my eye out!"

I led him out of the cubicle. "Your eye is fine. Here. Sit down." I picked a few pieces of glass out of his shaggy hair and tossed them back by the other pieces. "Looks like you have a few cuts. Nothing serious."

"Easy for you to say." He flopped backward onto the floor, and lay with both hands on his head. I think he was more shaken up than hurt. I know *I* was shaken up. Someone else probably was too. I turned back to the cubicle.

"Reginald? Are you okay in there?" Bits of glass tumbled off the chair as I pulled it out of the broken wall. One entire panel had completely shattered, and the blinds now hung by a thread. When I touched them, they fell off, and I tossed them aside. Cautiously—watching every foot placement—I stepped through the opening and into the cubicle. "Sorry. We didn't mean to . . ."

My words died in my throat. My entire body shivered, and not because I was only wearing swimming trunks. A massive guy stood inside the glass cubicle. He was old, probably seventeen. His breath came out fast and hard, and he stared at the broken glass covering the floor with a tight, twisted expression.

"Um . . . where's Reginald?" I asked.

The big guy's eyes snapped to my face at my last word. *It couldn't be. Could it?*

"Reginald?" He took one step toward me and then hesitated and stopped before his next one. Behind him, the three huge computer monitors laid out across his desk were covered with numbers and code way more complicated than anything I'd ever seen. I noticed he didn't have blinds on his side walls. Giant whiteboards stretched the entire length and width of both of them, each covered with multicolored numbers forming mathematical equations too complicated for even me—a certified math geek—to guess what he was trying to work out. How could this football jock of a guy be the reclusive ultranerd Reginald? I remembered the computer file. "Brock?"

His eyes lit up with a spark of recognition.

"You're Brock Reginald," I said.

"It's not . . . a good . . . idea . . . to let . . . them see . . . me."

"Are you feeling all right, Brock?" I took a couple of steps toward him.

"Stay by . . . myself."

"Sorry about this mess. It was an accident." One more step.

"Don't let . . . them see . . . me."

"It's okay, Brock. We want to be your friends. Right,   201

Coop?" I took three faster steps as Coop moaned and raised one hand straight up in the air, waving his pointer finger in agreement.

"You see . . . me!"

"Do you like Brock or Reg—" The last word and my breath were suddenly, violently cut off. The back of my head slammed into the hard surface of one of the whiteboards, and I had the odd thought that at least he hadn't shoved me through another glass panel. Giant, strong fingers clamped tight around my neck.

I tried to call out, but without any air, no words came. I jabbed at the choking hands. My wimpy fingers against those rock-hard sausages were like gnats bumping against the side of an elephant. Spots of blackness faded in and out in front of my eyes. My lungs cramped, shooting pain through my entire chest cavity.

Some part of me was aware of Coop yelling and whaling on Reginald, but he was only a fly against that elephant. The black spots took over completely.

And then . . . air. I sucked it in with huge, thirsty gulps. I was crumpled on the ground now, on all fours and not caring that my hands and knees were pressing against bits of broken glass. When I could think about something other than the joys of oxygen inside my lungs, I realized that Coop was sitting next to me. A gorilla guard had hold of Brock Reginald by the shoulders.

I lifted one arm, pointing. "He . . . tried to . . ." I had to stop to breathe.

"I know, man. He was killing you. He'd have done it too, if the guard dude hadn't pulled him off."

"He should . . . jail."

"Yeah, I don't like the idea of a crazy killer living with us either. Freak-out, isn't it, that old Reginald ends up looking like that."

Blond Gorilla Guard had Reginald settled in his chair, back in front of his computers.

"Calm down. Sit still," the guard told him.

"Hey, guard dude, Matt man here and I think this guy should be hauled off to jail. Or to the loony bin, at least."

"You two. Go to your rooms. Medical personnel will be up shortly to examine you."

"What about . . ." I climbed partway to my feet but had to take a break with my upper body leaning over on my thighs. "What about him?"

"He'll be fine. He just needs to get back to his work."

"No way, man. You can't just leave him loose on the top floor."

"Yeah, that's like letting a lion roam around." I brushed away the glass sticking to my hands and knees. Somehow I'd lucked out and hadn't gotten shredded. "How do we know he won't attack us again?"

"He won't because I said he won't!" The guard advanced on us a few steps. Coop and I scurried out of the cubicle like rats. "The two of you stay away from him; don't come near his cubicle. Then he won't touch you again. Got it?"

"Got it." I cowered behind Coop. One attack a day was plenty.

Coop nudged me toward the door to the bedroom hallway. "This is so skewed, bro." Turning, and walking backward, he pointed a cocky finger at the gorilla guard. "You're a total brain-fry, man. Total. This whole workhouse is fried!"

"Get going to your rooms! It's okay, Reginald, settle down. You're fine now. Here, you need to look at your computer screen. Look right there. That's right. Keep watching while I clean this up."

Some man—I don't know whether he was a doctor or not—came into my room and gave me the once-over. Besides some bruising and a few cuts I hadn't noticed before, I checked out fine. By the time Coop and I retrieved our floating island, Reginald was tucked tight back in his cubicle—the broken panel replaced by a tall sheet of plywood.

CHAPTER 20

"HE'S A PSYCH CASE." COOP'S VOICE boomed throughout the wide-open spaces of the pool room. I dodged an attempted blow from Jeffery's padded paddle and bent and strained my legs to keep my balance. "That's why they keep him shut away by himself. Any time he sees another human being, the dude tries to kill him."

"He didn't try to kill the guard." I twisted my head around to aim my voice toward Coop, who sat on the end of the diving board, dangling his feet in midair and waiting to play the winner.

Pow. I got in a good hit on Jeffery's upper arm. He made a low squeaking noise and then let out a banshee wail as he swung wildly in my general direction. Poor little guy. He didn't have a chance, especially since he was forced to take his glasses off so they wouldn't get broken. I jabbed him in the middle, not putting any-where near my full strength into it.

"The guard's got him trained—slips him raw steaks every night, just to get on his good side."

"Whatever." I braced against a hit to my hip and realized bracing was better than dodging for keeping my balance. "It's just—all those muscles. Doesn't he look exactly like the typical dumb jock? The guys we used to run away from in gym but ridicule in math and science."

"Totally. That dude could be the high school football team all by himself."

"He could bench-press the entire football team." Lifting my paddle, I blocked an attack from Jeffery. "Bench-press. Hey, Coop! I just figured it out. Those sounds we heard coming from Reginald's room. He's lifting weights in there."

"Could be, my brilliant top-floor bro. You two going to pussyfoot all day? When are you going to get serious about battling it out?"

Good question. I couldn't bring myself to smack Jeffery off his floating island, but I also couldn't *let* him knock me off.

The *bang-boing* sound behind me let me know that Coop had stood up on the diving board and was getting ready to jump.

"Double backflip this time, suckers. Watch and drool."

"Forget it, loser." I twisted the top half of my body around to watch, twirling my paddle over my head like it was a baton on steroids. "Don't even try."

He came down hard and two-footed on the end of the diving board, then instantly sprang into the air, throwing his arms up and tucking into a sort of ball. He hadn't gotten nearly enough air. He didn't even finish one flip, and it was sloppy and too close to the board. Way too close. With a crack that made me clench my teeth, the back of Coop's head smacked against the end of the diving board. My paddle slipped through my fingers, conking me on the head as it fell to my feet. The next second a big ball of vinyl-covered padding swung straight into the side of my face. It wasn't a hard hit, but I hadn't expected it, and it was enough to knock me off balance. As my arms flailed through the air, trying to grab on to anything to steady myself, my feet got tangled in my own paddle.

"Oh, wow, sorry." I heard Jeffery's voice before the water closed over me. I was only under a second or two. He was next to me, in the water, when I surfaced. "Sorry," he said again. "It was too late to stop the momentum of my swing when Coop hit the board. Hurry!"

Hurry?

Coop! I couldn't see him.

Even though he had a head start on me, I beat Jeffery to the deep end of the pool. I found Coop hanging from the silver ladder by one arm. His eyes were closed, and his whole face was scrunched up tight.

"Coop? Can you hear me?"

"Dude. Ow."

"Come on, you gotta get out of the pool."

Jeffery scrambled up the steps, and with me pushing from below, we heaved and pulled Coop onto dry ground. He sat still for a long while, his head resting on his knees and both hands deep in his shaggy hair.

"Can you walk yet?" My hands hovered near the back of his shoulders, unsure what they should do.

"Headache. Never had one like this before."

"We could help you to your bed," I said. "Maybe we should call that medical person to come back up and check you out again."

"Man, I've lived here for three months and never laid eyes on the dude. Now I'm seeing him twice in one week."

"Twice in one *day*," I corrected.

He peeked one eye open at me, smiling that goofy smile of his. "Bro, you're going to have to reboot me. We've got a system-wide hard-drive crash here. You're going to have to reprogram my brain."

Jeffery laughed so hard you'd think he'd never heard anything so funny in his entire life.

Something about what Coop said struck me wrong. It didn't sound funny to me at all.

• • •

It took a while for Jeffery and me to get Coop into his room. We bailed out of there fast when the medical man came in. Jeffery went back to the pool to practice his jousting moves. I changed and wandered into the rec room. One conk on the head was my daily limit.

I sat in a video rocker chair and stared up at the massive TV screen stretching across the wall in front of me. It didn't matter that I could barely hear the words coming from the set because of all the racket Kia and Isaac were making in the corner with their new pinball machine.

Someone sat down in the recliner close to me. I didn't blink.

"Is the remote broken?" a soft voice asked after a few minutes.

I glanced down at the black rectangle sitting in my hand, then back at the big screen. "I don't think so."

"Then why are you watching this?" she asked, so quietly I almost couldn't make out her words.

The images on the screen came into focus, revealing one of those stupid, half-hour-long infomercials that pretend to be real TV shows. A ditzy lady and an older man practically did backflips over a kitchen gizmo they claimed would change the world.

"Do you care?" the girl asked. I looked over and realized it was Paige.

209

"What?" I asked. She'd spoken so softly—and I'd been paying so little attention—her words hadn't registered.

"If I change the channel. Do you care?"

"No." I rocked way back in the chair and stared at the ceiling. Ten-second snatches of conversations filtered to my ears as Paige flipped through the channels. After a few minutes the remote landed on my stomach.

"There's nothing good on," she said. "You can have it back."

I raised my arm high enough to aim the remote and click off the TV. Paige didn't move—I could tell even without looking at her. Why was she just sitting there?

She started tapping her fingers against the armrests of the recliner. It was made of leather, so the sound came out loud and sharp.

Tap-tap-tap-tap-tap-tap-tap. It drowned out the dings and bells from Kia and Isaac at the pinball machine in the corner. *Tap-tap-tap.* Burrowing into my brain. *Tap-tap-tap-tap-tap-tap-tap.*

I sprang out of the chair.

"Will you knock it off?" I said, glaring down at her.

"Oh." She slid her hands into her lap and lowered her head. "Sorry. I'm just . . . bored."

"Go find your little buddy, Madeline. I'm sure she has a new outfit for you to squeal over." I sank back into the video rocker chair and, once again, stared at the ceiling.

"She's . . . doing something," she said.

"Watch a movie. Play video games. Go swimming. There's a ton of things you could do."

"I've done them all before. Watched them all. Played them all."

"Go do whatever it is Madeline is doing." Having her sit, doing nothing, so close to me put a serious kink in the nothingness I was trying to achieve.

"I can't," she said.

"Sure you can. She'll let you. She doesn't have any-one else to hang out with."

Paige made a gasping hiccup sound that made me look at her. Tears filled her eyes, then started dribbling out, one by one. *Great.* I let my head roll back. *I'm a jerk. I made her cry.* What had I said? Did she think I meant that Madeline only hung out with her because, now that Neela was gone, she really didn't have another choice? Or maybe Madeline really wouldn't let her hang out with her right now. That was probably it. They were having a fight. Girls did that all the time. I've seen it with Lauren. Best friends who can't spend five seconds apart get mad and decide they hate each other. It lasts for a day, a year, or an hour. Then they're back connected at the hip again. Don't ask me to understand.

211

"You know, I bet if you went and talked to her, you could work out whatever . . . problem you two are having."

"No. It's not that. Not really. It's just—if we were back home, Madeline and I would *never* choose each other as best friends."

Huh. Would Coop and I hang out together—out in the real world? Probably not. My main buds had been math and computer fanatics like Brennan and Lester. Coop wouldn't go with the total muscle heads, but he'd definitely find a group of jocks to spend his hours with.

Paige started sniffing big-time. "I just miss my family so much. I *hate* being stuck in here—unlike some people, like Madeline."

"And Jeffery," I added.

"Do you know what she's doing right now? She's having a *spa day*. Can you believe it? She turned our dance room into her own private spa, spending tons of money to have the lighting redone and furniture brought in. It's totally irresponsible." Her voice grew louder and faster. I'd never heard her speak so much, and she wasn't even finished. "She brought in a masseuse, and a pricey hairstylist, plus another person to do her nails. It's costing her an absurd amount of money, and she doesn't even care."

She glanced over at me and bit her lip. I think she'd

forgotten I was there. All these thoughts had been accu-
mulating inside her like raindrops in a bucket. She just
realized she'd dumped the whole thing over my head.

"At least it will soon be over," she said in that quiet
voice I was more accustomed to hearing from her. "I
won't have to listen to her talk about it anymore, and I
won't have to keep telling her that I'm not interested in
going in on it with her. Madeline has been working on
this project for more than a month now. It takes a long
time to get approval to bring outsiders up to the top
floor, longer than getting approval to go outside."

"We need approval to go outside?" I shook my ankle
bracelet at her and spoke with more sarcasm than was
necessary. "I thought we were free to go anywhere we
wanted."

She snapped her mouth shut, staring at my ankle,
and sank deep into her chair.

My foot came down. "Maybe Madeline and Jeffery
have the right idea. What difference is it going to make
how much we spend in here? Our parents certainly don't
care how far over the limit we are, so why should we?"

Her voice dropped to an even quieter mouse-
whispering level. "My parents care. I care."

"Your parents care? I don't think so, or you wouldn't
be here."

"They couldn't help it. My little brother . . . he's   213 always been really sick. . . . All the hospital bills . . . They couldn't help it. My dad took on another job, and I came here. We're all working hard so we can get back under the limit."

"Sure. That's what they tell you, so you'll go along quietly. They raise our families' limits as soon as we come here. Perfect excuse for them to go shopping and pile up even more debt."

She shook her head, unbelieving. "Maybe your parents, but mine—"

"What's so different about yours? Huh? You think your parents love you more? They don't! They're all the same."

She blew out a disgusted breath as she pushed herself out of her chair. "You've been sitting in front of the TV too long. It's scrambled your brains."

"It's true," I said, shooting myself in the head with a finger gun. "Total system meltdown. You're going to have to reboot me, just like Coop. Reprogram my brain."

Reprogram my brain.

Staring at the big blank screen in front of me, everything suddenly clicked into place, like sliding that last blue Rubik's Cube square into position. "Oh. My. Gosh."

Lauren's voice: *My work is weird. I mean, I don't even know how to do it. Still, I have to sit in my little chair and stare*
at the computer screen for four hours every day. It's really stupid.

Blond Gorilla Guard: *It's okay, Reginald, settle down. You're fine now. Here, you need to look at your computer screen. Look right there. That's right. Keep watching while I clean this up.*

The headaches. Seizures.

They were doing something to us, sending some sort of electrowaves into our brains while we worked on our computers. They were reprogramming our brains without us even knowing about it.

"Paige, wait! Don't leave. I think I just figured something out."

"That you're a rude jerk?" She folded her arms across her chest with a huff, but she did stop and turn toward me. "You're not very bright for a Top Floor, are you? I figured that out weeks ago."

"You're right. I am a jerk. I'm sorry. Maybe your parents aren't like mine, but listen. I think I just realized what they're doing to us in here."

"Who's doing what to whom?"

"The FDRA. Miss Smoot. Everyone here. To us kids."

"What do you mean?" Her arms fell out of that tight cross, and her fingers twisted together.

"I'm not sure of the details, but I've got the general idea." I jumped to my feet and started pacing in small circles. "I've got to find out. It'd be on their computer,

215

but I don't know if I can access it fast enough." The band around my ankle suddenly felt ten times as heavy. The security guards had most likely started watching my computer activity extra closely after my blanking-out-the-monitors trick. Once they realized I was hacking again, they'd shut me down fast. I couldn't do this alone. I grabbed Paige by the wrist and pulled her out the rec room door. "Come on, let's go find Coop and Jeffery. We need help."

CHAPTER 21

"BUT WHAT IF WE FIND SOMETHING incriminating?" Jeffery asked. Paige and I sat cross-legged on the floor with him in a corner of the gym. At the moment it was the best place for a private meeting. Madeline's spa filled up the dance room. Kia and Isaac were still dinging and pinging on their pinball machine in the rec room. The pool room was too humid, and the cubicles were too exposed.

"We'll figure how to get a copy of it to outside authorities once we do," I said.

"No. I mean, what happens to us? Will things change around here? Will we have to move out of the workhouse?"

Oh, yeah. Jeffery didn't want to go home. Ever.

"To be honest, I don't know." I ran the tip of my finger back and forth on the glossy wood floor in front of me. "I don't know what we're going to find for sure, and I don't know what it will mean. I do know this— I'd rather find out the truth about what is going on around here, no matter what the consequences are."

"I guess," he said, not sounding very convinced. Just how bad *had* his home life been?

"Jeffery." Paige's soft voice came out a lot more confident than usual. "Do you remember about three months ago—when Miss Smoot sent us an e-mail telling us we were no longer allowed to order any meals from Lily Gardens Chinese Restaurant?"

"She never did tell us why," said Jeffery with a grumble.

Paige giggled. "Maybe she got a bad fortune cookie from them."

"They took the link off the workhouse home page and put up blocks." Jeffery explained to me. He twitched his eyebrows. "I got through anyway. It wasn't easy, but I did it. I ordered Lily Gardens food every day for a week."

"I remember seeing fresh cartons of untouched Chinese food in the rec room at lunch and dinnertime," she said. "You probably would have ordered it for breakfast if they'd been open that early."

"Yeah." His eyes were focused on something outside the circle the three of us made. His smile flattened out. "The receptionist finally caught on to where the food deliveries were coming from and blocked them from being brought up."

"That's not the point." Paige's voice grew even stronger. "Obviously you don't even like Chinese food, but you kept ordering it just because Miss Smoot told you not to."

Now I could see where this was going. *Keep at it, Paige. You're almost there.*

He let out a small grunt, and his smile came back. "Yeah. It was sort of like a dare."

"This is the same thing," said Paige, "but much more important than Lily Gardens Restaurant. This has to do with right and wrong. It's a dare too. A challenge. We're the good guys on a dangerous mission to stop the bad guys."

"Kind of like a game." He sat up straight, his eyes bright. "And you want me to play it with you?"

"We're begging you to play," I said.

"Okay. I'm in. What's the plan?"

I popped Paige softly on her thigh with the side of my fist, and she did the same back to me in our own silent *Yes!*

I scooted in to make a tighter circle. "I need some help figuring out the details, but here's what I thought we could do . . ."

One forty-one a.m. A perfectly random time. No one would suspect. If everything went as planned, Jeffery would leave his room in exactly five minutes. I hoped he'd remembered to set his alarm. I didn't end up needing mine. I couldn't sleep. Coop had been out of it the entire evening, after his head-banging diving accident, so we'd been forced to move ahead without him.

Paige met me at the door to the hallway. Her whole body shivered.

"You okay?" I asked.

She nodded.

"Did you bring the lighter?"

"Of course."

After my last escape Honey Lady had ordered a search of my room and cubicle and confiscated the lighter. She'd made a new rule that the girls had to keep their butane candle lighters in their bedrooms—stashed in a spot inaccessible to me. She'd never counted on me turning Paige into a rebel.

"You don't have to do this." I said. "After we set off the smoke detector, you can sneak back to your room. I can cause a distraction by myself."

She hesitated for a second then shook her head. "I'm all right. Let's stick with this plan. It's the most believable."

I breathed in deeply and nodded. "Let's go."

The instant we walked into the hallway to the stairs, we heard the ding of the elevator arriving on the top floor.

Crud. Had they noticed me moving around so quickly because of my ankle monitor? I thought it only gave the alarm when I took my first step off the top floor. The guards had probably picked us up on the video monitors because no other kids in the entire workhouse were moving around. But getting caught right now didn't fit with the plan. It was too early. I thought we'd have a minute or two before a guard got to us. We couldn't let him catch us yet. Jeffery hadn't even left his room.

Paige and I didn't have time to set off the smoke detector before the elevator door opened. The only thing we could do was dart back into the cubicle room. We couldn't get caught here, though. Jeffery needed to be alone. I just hoped I was right about my ankle monitor not showing a blip on their screen while I was on the top floor. Otherwise we'd be shut down before we started.

"Come on," I whispered to Paige as we stared at the dark work area. The two of us slipped inside Jeffery's cubicle—just because it wasn't the first or second one. Either of those would have been too obvious.

Please let there be only one guard on duty this late at night. I hadn't looked that far into the guard schedule back on my first day at the workhouse when I'd hacked into it. If an extra guard was watching our every movement, we wouldn't be hiding long.

The door from the stair hall made a click as the guard entered the work area. Jeffery had stored a big pile of boxes in his cubicle. Paige and I silently slid some of them in front of us. We stopped breathing and ducked even closer to the ground when a shaft of light shined around the corner. The beam hit the boxes and the wall above our heads, but we remained undetected. We breathed slowly and softly as the guard moved on to Coop's cubicle.

Seconds zoomed by. Jeffery was going to walk out here any moment now and crash right into the guard. *Come on. Hurry and finish your inspection and get off this floor!*

Finally we heard the door to the elevator hall open and close. We remained hidden for several more minutes, just to make sure the guard had really left. Shoving the boxes aside, we pushed ourselves to our feet and hurried toward the stairs.

Where was Jeffery? He should have been out here ages ago. If I had to take the time to go wake him up, the guard would make it back downstairs to the monitoring room and see us before we got where we needed to go.

Jeffery came out of the boys' hallway right as Paige and I ran past it. He must have noticed the guard and waited in his room to avoid him. I should've had more faith in the little guy. He was no dummy.

We gave each other knowing nods and headed in different directions.

"You can do it, Jeffery." It was too dark to see for sure, but I could just imagine the worried look on his face. He'd been assigned the job as hacker tonight, searching the workhouse's files and getting us the cold hard facts we needed. We hadn't had a choice, even though both of us would have loved for me to be the one doing the online breaking and entering. The ankle monitor made the decision. We needed every adult in the building to barrel down on *me* and leave Jeffery alone to mess with the files. He was unsure, but I knew he could get in and get the info we wanted. He had some amateur hacking abilities—he'd been able to order the forbidden Chinese food—and I'd worked with him for more than two hours before lights-out, showing him tricks on some "safe" small-business and personal sites. I'd also written out what I already knew about hacking into the workhouse site from my previous break-ins. With that head start, he should be good to go—that is, if our assumption was right. Palge had said she was almost positive the computers in the cubicle room did not shut down at lights-out like our bedroom computers. If they did, we had no hope. We were also hoping that—if the guard noticed computer activity at all—he'd be much less alarmed, and slower to take a closer look, when he realized Jeffery was logged in and not me.

223

After setting off the smoke detector and quickly fanning away the whiffs to make it stop beeping, Paige and I took the stairs down to the fourth floor and walked into the dark, quiet cubicle area. We took a deep breath. We'd made it. *Come on up and get us, guard. Now's the time.* I checked my ankle monitor. The normal, constant yellow light on the side had changed to a bright blue light flashing in hypertime. The longer we could distract the guard, though, the more time we gave Jeffery.

Paige and I looked at each other in the dim glow of the security lights. My heart thumped at what we were about to do. Maybe this wasn't such a good idea.

"Here?" I asked Paige.

"Okay. But . . ." Her voice trailed off, and she stared at her shoes.

"But what?"

"It's just . . ." She lifted her head and crinkled her nose. "It doesn't seem very natural. You know?"

"Oh." I gulped. "What would seem natural?"

"The rec room?" she said with a single-shoulder lift.

"Okay." My voice came out with a squeak. Maybe the guard would catch us before we got there.

Whose idea had this distraction been anyway? Oh, yeah. Mine. I was excited at the time I thought it up. Stupid.

We edged our way into the rec room.

"Should we turn on the lights?" I asked.

"We could, but . . ."

"It wouldn't seem natural," I finished for her. "Why go to all the trouble to sneak down here and then blow it by turning on the lights? It's too dark, though." The rec room didn't have safety lighting like the halls. "The guard needs to be able to see us. We have to turn on something."

"What about the television?" asked Paige.

"That might work." I turned on the big screen—not nearly as big or new as ours on the top floor—and flipped it to a music video channel. A television set can give off an amazing amount of light in a dark room. Should do the trick. Time to move on with the plan.

I shot Paige a glance. She looked away fast and sat down on the sofa, balancing so close to the edge of the cushion, I thought she'd slip off. Her hands made a tight knot in her lap.

I sat down next to her—but not too close. *You can come now, guard. Anytime.* We had to give him something to concentrate on when he got here.

"Okay," I said. "Ready?"

Paige nodded, but leaned away from me.

I sucked in a deep breath. "Okay."

I raised my arm and moved it behind her back, not exactly sure what I was supposed to do with it. I let my hand drop onto her shoulder. Her cheeks turned pink. Mine were probably a deep, dark red.

She closed her eyes and whispered, "It's just the plan. The plan, the plan." She didn't seem to be talking to me. I think she was trying to pump herself up.

"He'll be here any second," I said in a low voice. Where was he, anyway? Had he taken a pit stop in the restroom on his way back to the monitoring room? Soon, though. The second he heard the alarm set off by my ankle monitor he'd fly up here and stop us. It just had to *look* as if we'd sneaked down to the fourth floor to make out. I didn't know why anyone would go to a different floor to do that, but we hoped the guard would be too upset to think that part through.

I moved close, stretching out with my lips. She leaned in toward me.

Wait a minute. Wasn't I supposed to close my eyes or something? If I did, I wouldn't know where her mouth was. How did people do this? I'd just have to keep my eyes open.

And then our lips touched. Pop! Just like that it was over and we pulled back. Where was the guard? He hadn't made it in time. Oh, well. I leaned toward Paige again. Guess we'd have to keep kissing.

A bright light flashed in my eyes. I sprang at least three feet down the sofa away from Paige.

"Whoa, dude! What are you . . . ? Oh, man, bro, oh, man!" Bursts of laughter came out with Coop's words.

I jumped to my feet. "What are you doing here?"

"Me? Bro, I think you're the one who should answer that question." Coop walked closer, holding the lantern he used at night right in my face.

"Did you follow me?" I asked, shielding my eyes.

"Every step of the way, and I must say I'm disappointed. A girl? Is she why you abandoned me in my room, injured and possibly dying?"

"No, of course not. You weren't dying, and I don't even like her."

A little *erp* came out of Paige.

I turned toward her. "I mean, I like you fine. I just don't . . ."

She slid her head forward until her hair covered her face. Man, I screwed up big-time. Why did I always say such stupid things to her? I didn't mean to hurt her feelings.

"I like you," I said, lowering my voice. "I really do. You're cool. It's just that before today I didn't even know you, really. You know?"

"I know," she said in a barely recognizable whisper. "It was all part of the plan. I know."

I knew too, but for some reason I couldn't stop thinking about that kiss.

Before any of us could say anything else, the dark space behind Coop got a lot darker. Goatee Gorilla Guard had come into the room, hulking and breathing hard.

"Don't yell," I said fast. "The Fourth Floors are all asleep down here. You don't want to wake them up."

"Get . . . back . . . to . . . your . . . rooms." His voice was low and controlled. Barely controlled. We bolted.

A piece of paper had been slipped under my bedroom door. I snatched it up fast and took it into the closet to read with a flashlight. It was from Jeffery.

Got it. We'll take a look tomorrow.

CHAPTER 22

THE INSTANT LUNCH BREAK BEGAN, we sprinted to the rec room. Forget about eating; we had more important things to do.

"Where'd the machine come from?" Coop asked.

"I've got half a dozen of them in my room," said Jeffery.

"You didn't have any problem getting them through package screening?" asked Paige. "Sometimes the guards can be stinkers about electronic devices."

"Why would they care about blank laptops?" asked Jeffery. "They don't have anything dangerous on them. There's no wireless Internet in the building, so I can't download anything they don't want me to. It's a totally unconnected machine—which is one of the reasons I've never pulled it out of its box before."

"And why we're using it instead of one of our other computers. We can't let any of the monitors know what we're doing. Jeffery turned this laptop into a lethal weapon. It now holds all the files full of incriminating evidence he copied onto a flash drive last night. Coop, every few minutes jump out of your chair and yell, so the guards will think we're playing a video game if they happen to see us on the monitor."

He jumped into the air immediately, pumping his fist. "Wa-hoo!"

"Uh, Coop, it might be better if we were actually looking at the computer first. Matt, here's the flash drive I used." Jeffery handed me the black plastic rectangle, and I stuck it deep inside my front pocket.

"Thanks, Jeffery."

The four of us scrunched around the laptop at a table. Paige sat off to one side while Coop, Jeffery, and I huddled in front of it. No one else was in the rec room. We needed the privacy. Meeting in one of our bedrooms would've eliminated the chances of another Top Floor walking in on us, but then Paige wouldn't have been able to come. She deserved to see what Jeffery had copied as much as anyone. More than Coop, actually.

"What exactly are we looking for, bro?" Coop asked.

"Anything that has to do with headaches or seizures—I'll do a search using one of those words in a minute." My eyes scanned the names of the displayed files. "We've also got to find something about how they're beaming information into our brains through the computer."

"I don't like the idea of getting my brain zapped every day." Coop shook out his shaggy hair. "It's zapped enough as it is."

I had to smile as my eyes flicked across the screen. "I won't argue with you on that one." I clicked on a folder labeled *Outside Communication*. If the information being fed into our brains came from outside the workhouse, the folder seemed likely to be the one we wanted. We found files on each kid in the workhouse. I clicked Jeffery's first, but it was blank inside.

"Always knew there was nothing going on inside you, bro," Coop said, reaching around me to nudge Jeffery on the back of his head. "Try me next."

Coop's file was full of messages, copies of e-mails to and from his parents.

"Hey," he said, leaning close. "Hey!"

We were all realizing the same thing at the same time. This file contained original e-mail messages followed by edited, altered, or completely rewritten drafts.

"I knew it!" Coop said, almost happy. "I told you the messages from my parents sounded stiff, didn't I? See, read here. They're cool. They've got a sense of humor." His voice suddenly got cold. "Those FDRA jerks were trying to cut me off, weren't they?"

"They don't want us to care about any life other than what we have on the top floor." My teeth ground together so hard I wouldn't have been surprised if they'd cracked. I opened my own file. The first line read, *Technical Difficulties Simulated*. The next line said, *Block Lifted* and a date—the date I escaped and went home. I found a concerned message from my dad that he had sent that very night, explaining the family's financial situation and apologizing for the mistakes he and Mom had made and his plans to fix the situation. His plans weren't much better than Mom's, but I could tell that both my parents loved me and were doing the best they could. The rewritten FDRA version of Dad's e-mail, the one that I'd received, was also in the file.

"This makes me so mad I can hardly think," I said, closing down the folder. "Let's move on to something else."

"Right," said Coop, dragging out his words. "Because we know everything else we find is going to make us so-o-o happy."

"Hey! Look in that one," yelled Jeffery. His finger pointed to a folder labeled simply *Profit*. I clicked on it. "It was really hard to get. But I did what you told me to, Matt, and I got it. You said the hardest files to get to are the ones you want. What's that document you're reading? What does it say?"

"It's some sort of a contract." My eyes skimmed over the endless lines of tiny words. "Someone is paying the workhouse to do something."

"Ooooh, big surprise," said Coop, wiggling his fingers and bugging out his eyes. "That's the whole point of this place, fool. Companies pay us to do work all the time."

"I think . . . this is something else." I'd gotten deeper into the contract, and I wasn't comfortable with what I was reading. "This is a big contract. For dozens and dozens of kids." I sat back a bit, letting out a long breath. "I can't find where it says what the contracted work is."

"Let's go look at those other files in the folder," said Jeffery, practically bouncing in his chair.

Each file—and there were scores of them—was labeled with a child's name.

"Ho-ly. Cow." I couldn't believe what I was reading.

"No way, dude," said Coop. "That has to be like illegal or something. Doesn't it?"

"I said it from the beginning. They're reprogramming our brains."

"Treating us like lab rats is more like it," said Paige, her soft voice edged with anger.

"It's an interesting concept, anyway," said Jeffery. "Modifying behavior, implanting knowledge."

"Too bad it can have side effects like . . ." I pointed to a line at the bottom of a Second Floor's file. "Severe headaches." I exited out of that file and found Lauren's. "And here, mild seizure."

233

"Not everyone gets them," said Paige. "I wonder why not."

"Maybe that's part of the experiment," I said, disgust thick in my voice. "Find out what makes some people susceptible."

"Neela started getting really bad headaches," said Paige. Last night I'd told the others about Neela still being at the workhouse, but on the fourth floor. I hadn't really thought about her much since I saw her, with everything else that had happened. It was only when Paige and I discussed sneaking down to the fourth floor as part of our plan that I remembered Neela was there.

"No one else on the top floor has. Statistically, we should be the same as the other floors. About a fourth of us should be getting them." I searched around for the Top Floors' files and learned an interesting fact. Of all the remaining Top Floors, only one of us had a file. Brock Reginald.

Coop punched the air with his fist. "Yes. I told you. I knew there was something off about that dude. He really is a dumb muscle head. They just programmed him to be supersmart and moved him up here with the rest of us geniuses."

"And also programmed him to stay out of sight, so we wouldn't get suspicious. Interesting. I wonder why

he's the only one who became a superbrain."

"Just like the headache thing, bro. People respond differently. The dude was an anomaly whose brain accepted the info-dumping to the max."

"The rest of us Top Floors don't get experimented on, because we're valuable." I rubbed one finger up and down the side of my jaw as I stared at the screen. "We're smart, and we make enough money doing our work. They don't want to mess with *our* brains."

Paige sucked in a sharp gasp of air. "Neela. She was really struggling with her work. And then . . ." Her voice choked up. "Her family never did get under their limit, did they? Miss Smoot lied to us."

I nodded. "Right. They just started reprogramming Neela's brain and dropped her down to the fourth floor as soon as it was obvious the info dump on her hadn't worked."

"This sucks, man," said Coop. "They better be making a bundle off all those poor robot-brain kids."

"We can find out." It only took me a few seconds to bring up the workhouse's accounting files. "Yep. They're raking it in—not bothering to pass any along to the kids or their families, though. The company that's paying for the experiments must think this research is very valuable."

"Ew," said Paige in a shaky whisper. "I don't like the idea of a company developing technology to get into people's brains like that."

"It's not legal." I shook my head. "It can't be."

"Hey, bro, while we're in here, pull up my account. Let's see how much moola I'm pulling in. Database designers like me shouldn't come cheap."

I had to chuckle. Thanks goodness for Coop being around to lighten the mood.

"Whoa, dude, I'm rich," said Coop.

Smiling, I nodded. Each week a good chunk of cash was deposited into Coop's family's account thanks to him.

"But what . . . why are there so many deductions?" asked Paige, her voice squeaking as she struggled to raise it above her normal mouse-quiet level.

Scrunching his nose and pushing up his glasses, Jeffery leaned close to the screen. "Yeah—wow—look how much they took out of the account."

What the heck? They were charging us major bucks to live our luxurious lives on the top floor. Man, they made us pay for everything—including all the food and clothes we ordered. The room rental and housekeeping fees alone ate up a huge chunk of Coop's weekly payroll deposit—which would be similar to the rest of ours. Then the FDRA added charges like a pool maintenance fee. An extra power fee for all our electrical equipment. They even tacked on an extra fee for bringing deliveries all the way up to the top floor.

"Hey, who's the dude who gets the school tutorial fee?"

asked Coop, pointing to a line on the screen. "Nobody ever tutorialed me."

"Me either," I said, my voice gone dead.

"We need to ask for a refund, bro."

We needed to ask a lot of things.

"Why didn't I see any of this when I pulled up my family's account back home?"

"Check it out," said Jeffery. "Deposits are made into our families' accounts weekly, but withdrawals are only posted every month. The money is taken out daily, but they wait and post it all together at the end of that month. You haven't been here long enough, Matt."

"What kind of wacko accounting system is that?" asked Coop.

"One that keeps our families in the dark until it's too late for them to do anything about it," I said.

"I've been here long enough," said Paige. "My parents would've seen the deductions by now. Why didn't they tell me?"

"Maybe they don't want you to worry." I remembered how hard she said her family was working to get back under their limit. "Maybe once the FDRA gets us here, there's no way for our parents to get us out. Or maybe your parents tried to tell you, but their e-mails got blocked. Or it just might be that your parents never look at their account statement. Lots of people don't." 237

"They look," said Paige.

"My parents never look," said Coop. "They'd rather live in ignorant la-la land. How do you think I ended up in here in the first place?"

"Same with me." I pulled up my file. I dug deep to see how much had been taken out of my family's account. A huge batch of fees had been applied a week and a half ago—the day Lauren was taken. I'd have to go back and check Coop's file again to be sure, but I didn't remember seeing such a large amount taken from his account at one time. It made me wonder if someone had noticed how smart I was and decided they needed another Dunston sibling at the workhouse. Maybe the FDRA knew how smart I was before they took me in the first place. That might have been the "special circumstance" that caused them to bring me here instead of giving my family a choice of consequences for going over the limit.

The fees they charged me included a transportation fee, a hefty testing and training fee, and a first-night room fee so big I wanted to go back to the first floor and check to see if the sheets I'd slept between down there were spun from pure gold. Some of the blame for our family's financial mess still belonged to Mom and Dad, but not all of it. Not by a long shot.

"I bet hardly any of our parents realize how little of what we earn helps pay off the debt." I looked more closely at the numbers, adding them up quickly in my head. "In fact, look at this. It's worse, much worse. Even if we didn't order a single item online—including food— we don't make enough to cover the cost of living on the top floor."

"Shoot," said Jeffery. "So I don't really need to waste time buying all those expensive electronics?"

"Whoa. You mean after busting my butt here for three months, I've done nothing but improve my paddle-wall-ball skills and drain money from my family's account?"

A soft sob came from Paige's direction. Tears streaked down her face.

"Why?" I asked. "Why do they give us so much and then turn around and make us pay more for it? What good does that do? It's like . . . it's . . . like . . ."

My words trailed off as it hit me. It must have hit Coop at the same time.

"They want to keep us here as long as they can. They hope we never go home. We're like indentured servants. We're smart, bro, the smartest there are. They must be making major bucks off us. They don't have to pay us as much as adults get for the same work. It's all about the dollars, dude."

Kia and Isaac walked into the room and headed for the pinball machine. The four of us huddled closer to the computer.

"What are you dweebs so interested in over there?" asked Kia.

"Nothing," I said. I didn't want to explain what we'd learned to anyone else until I got a firm handle on it. We'd let Kia, Isaac, Madeline, and maybe—somehow— even Reginald know before long.

I lowered my voice to a whisper that barely registered over the bells and dings of the pinball machine. "It seems like they went to an awful lot of work just to keep what . . . eight kids up here?"

"Work they'd have to do anyway, because of Federal Debt Ordinance 169-D," said Jeffery. "Do you think they do the same thing at every workhouse?"

"Who knows," I said. "The only thing that matters to us is that the people at this one—the one we're stuck at—decided to make some extra money at our expense." I clicked back into Lauren's files. "Yeah, see, they don't give Third Floors as much nice stuff as we have, and they don't charge them anywhere near what they charge us. They don't care so much about keeping them." I checked a few random files of kids from different floors. The lower the floor, the lower the charges.

"Those second-floor dudes must be living in a dump," said Coop. "They don't have to pay hardly anything."

"They're no good to the FDRA," I said. "They want them to go home. In fact, maybe they *want* the lower-floor kids to rotate out. Maybe they need fresh brains to experiment on every so often. We Top Floors are valuable. They lie to us, make us think we're special. Make us think we're helping our families when all we're doing is dragging them deeper into debt. What the . . . look at that! They're charging us thirty percent interest on the amount we overspend—and we're all overspending after they deduct all those hiked-up fees. It's insane! Man, they hit pay dirt with us, didn't they?"

"Man," echoed Coop.

"And the poor kids who aren't smart enough to pull in the big bucks get turned into lab rats. *Money, money, money. Let's see how much money we can suck out of these kids before they drop over dead.*" A ball of angry emotion barreled up from my feet.

I picked up the chair I'd been sitting on and lifted it high over my head. With an anguished roar I ran over to the pinball machine and smashed the chair down on the smooth, horizontal surface. Glass shattered. Kia screamed. The pinball machine pinged.

"Whoa, dude," said Coop.

Isaac grabbed the front of my shirt and would have lifted me onto my toes if he'd been strong enough. "What'd you do that for, you little brat? I'm going to kill you, you know that?"

"Yeah? Go ahead." I stuck my nose defiantly in the 241

air. Despite his tough words, I knew he'd never try anything. He was too skinny to hurt me. Even if he could, what did I care?

"You little punk," said Isaac.

"Calm down. Back off." Kia's hands tugged backward on Isaac's shoulders, making him release me. "He'll make it right. He'll buy us a new one." She shot me a hot glare. "Won't you."

"Sure, why not? Who cares?" I said, shrugging my shirt back into place. "I'll buy you a hundred new ones. It doesn't matter. None of us are going to get out of here until we're eighteen anyway." My voice rose with fury. "No matter what we do, we're stuck here. Do you all realize that? They're making sure we never leave!"

I heard a muffled sob from Paige.

So what? Let her cry.

As I reached for another chair, four huge hands grabbed my upper arms. Gorilla Man and the goatee guard had ambushed me from behind. I kicked and twisted, even though I knew from experience that fighting back was pointless. A sharp prick in my hip took me by surprise. The room turned in circles around me, and everything got fuzzy. The one clear thing I saw before the blackness overwhelmed me was fingers with long, white nails. They closed the laptop and picked it up.

CHAPTER 23

CLICK! CLICK! CLICK! THE SHARP noise bored into my brain. *Click! Click! Click!* Like a gun misfiring, over and over again. *Click! Click! Click!* A gun pointed right at my head.

A hand slapped hard and insistently against the side of my leg.

"Wake up!"

I squinted open my eyes. *Augh!* Too much light. Rolling to my side, I pulled the limp pillow I'd been lying on over my face.

An even harder slap. "Now!"

"Sheesh! You're the one who knocked me out!" Pulling the pillow down, I gave it a good punch. She was lucky I didn't throw it at her.

"You were subdued for your own protection, as well as the protection of the other children in the room. No one is to blame for that except you."

"Right," I drawled. "The only thing you care about is protecting us little kids."

The clicking of her heels started up again as she paced back and forth at the foot of my bed. But wait, I wasn't really lying on a bed. Struggling, I sat up, unable to find a firm surface underneath me to push against. I was on a soggy cot, and four more cots were lined up to the side of mine. Where was I? The ceiling stretched high above me, unfinished, with pipes and ducts showing. A long folding screen, about seven feet high and I don't know how many feet long, ran behind Honey Lady, pretending to be a wall making a real room out of this space the cots occupied.

"What is this place?"

"You are on the first floor. This is our holding room for First Floors before they're taken away to their labor-oriented workhouses."

"You sure spent the big bucks on this floor, didn't you? And now you stuck me here. Hmm, wonder what that means."

Her eyes went wild. I braced myself for the feel of her nails scraping down the sides of my face. They didn't come, but I wouldn't have been surprised. "You will not speak to me in that tone. *I* am the head of this workhouse. It will be run in the manner I think best. Workhouse residents will do as *I* say. Do you have any idea the chaos you've created on the top floor?"

I pushed my back up against the wall behind me. I'd

never seen this side of Honey Lady before: a furious, on-the-brink-of-losing-control woman.

"How dare you upset those other children like that!"

How dare I? Who did she think she was? Let the fingernail scraping come. I didn't even care. "Oh, no. We can't have upset Top Floors, now, can we." Sarcasm gushed from me like water from the end of a hose. "If we upset the Top Floors, they're not going to be able to concentrate on their work. They're not going to be able to make as much money for the FDRA. We can't have that. If that goes on too long, we'll have to drop them down to the fourth floor, where we can start making money with them by performing dangerous experiments on their brains."

"Mr. Dunston, I don't know what you think you discovered when you *illegally* rifled through my computer files, but I assure you, you've misunderstood the information. I will not tolerate the insubordinate behavior you've displayed."

"Hang on, what I *think* I discovered? Listen, lady, I know exactly what I found, and I'm not going to let you get away with what you're doing to us kids in here anymore."

One last click and she stopped, square at the end of my cot, arms folded, chin high, narrowed eyes glaring down on me.

"Get up." Turning on her heel, she walked out of the folding-screen fake room. I swung my legs over the side of the cot and followed. We stepped into a wide, open area. One other long folding screen ran down the adjacent wall, which I assumed partitioned off the girls' cots. One First Floor guy sat in the far corner, watching TV. A girl sat drawing at one of the picnic-style tables in the middle of the room.

"Jessica, will you please go watch the television for a while?" Honey Lady asked, her voice momentarily reverting to its normal sugar-overdose tone. It turned back to all-business when she pulled out her cell phone. "Bring me the laptop."

"Interesting," I said, as I slid sideways onto a bench of the picnic table. "*Your* cell phone works fine in this building. It was all part of cutting us off, wasn't it? Fill our lives with never-ending fun and distractions. Eliminate or change any contact from former family and friends. Soon enough we'll forget about life off the top floor. We'll forget we didn't want to come here in the first place."

"Sit."

Crab Woman pushed through the metal industrial doors with a loud clang. Honey Lady snatched the laptop from her and dismissed her without saying a word.

"Now, Matthew, why don't you show me exactly what

it was you found that got you so riled up?" She lowered herself onto the bench next to me and scooted up close. She wasn't back to sticky-sweet, but she wasn't foaming at the mouth anymore either. "I'll see if I can explain the files to you, so you'll understand the truth of how we operate in this workhouse and can forget about the silly make-believe horror story you think you discovered."

"Fine." I tugged the computer in front of me. "I'd like to see what you come up with to explain away the *facts* I found."

I clicked. I searched. The files that Jeffery had downloaded, the files that had taken me less than a second to pull up in the rec room . . . were gone. I searched all over the place. They were nowhere. Deleted.

"You erased them."

Wrapping one arm softly around my shoulder, she leaned right up in my face and said, with as much innocence as a grandmother, "I erased what, sweetie?"

Shoving her arm away, I sprang to my feet. "The files! All the important files. The files with anything on them that mattered. You did it on purpose!" Stepping on the bench seat, I moved away from the picnic table. "You knew if I had a copy of them, you could be in trouble."

She opened her eyes extra wide, trying to look naive and innocent. "I really don't have any idea what you are talking about." 247

"You're doing things at this workhouse that are plain wrong, and you don't want anyone to find out. I'll bet none of the other workhouses hire out their kids as lab rats. They don't suck their Top Floors' accounts of every penny and then a whole lot more!"

"You have quite an imagination, you know. Maybe I should move you to a project that's based more on creativity."

"You can't erase my mind. I know what I saw! The other kids do too—Jeffery, Coop, and Paige. We'll tell. You won't get away with this!"

"Get away with what? As you can see, I have nothing to hide." She gestured to the laptop with a flat hand. "You could search every computer file in this entire building. You won't be able to find anything that would raise an eyebrow."

I kicked the curving metal tube that served as the table leg. "You've been busy while I was knocked out. You cleaned up all your files. Everywhere." I gave it another kick. "I don't care. I know. I have witnesses to back me up."

"Really? And just who are you going to tell?"

"Everyone! Our parents. The police. The FBI."

Smirking a little, she twitched her eyebrows.

"The news! TV reporters. They'd love a story like this."

"Sure they would, if you had the facts to back it up."

"The other kids will back me up."

Her smile grew more confident. "Why don't you go ahead and try to get your story out."

Shoot. No cell phone. Screened e-mail. I kicked out with my monitored ankle. No running away. There had to be some way. Eventually, I could hack through something and get word out. I *knew* I could. Unless they kept me locked down here on the no-tech first floor. I doubted that playing along, acting as if I were flowing happily with the program, would work again.

"Listen, Matt. Even if by some miracle you were able to get your *story* out, who's going to believe it? What reputable news company would publish a story that accuses a powerful government agency of such heinous crimes . . . without a single shred of proof other than the say-so of four kids? Add to that the fact that these kids are extremely bright, with records of causing trouble because they are bored with the humdrum life going on around them?"

Proof. I needed some solid, hard facts. Man! *If only we'd made another . . . copy.* Quickly, I turned my back on Honey Lady, so she couldn't read my expression. I didn't want to give anything away. My right hand slid casually into my front pocket. The files on the laptop had been the second copy. My fingers curled around the flash

249

drive in my pocket—the first copy. Releasing it, I pulled out my hand and turned back around.

Don't give anything away. "Someone would believe us! I know it."

One side of her mouth lifted in a smirking smile. "Go ahead and try."

I let all the air gush out of my lungs, and slumped back down on the picnic table bench, hunched and defeated. At least that was the look I was going for. She seemed to buy it and snuggled up close to me again with that arm around my shoulder.

"Life can be very good here at the workhouse for a boy as smart as you. Why don't you just decide to enjoy it?"

With my head hanging low, I shrugged. My mind raced. Somehow I had to get that flash drive out of the workhouse. It had to get into the hands of someone who could do something about it—who could expose what Honey Lady was doing to the world.

"You really don't have any other choice, you know," she said.

I sniffed, hoping it sounded as if I were trying not to cry. "I know."

"Are you willing to give it another try? Will you leave your imagined stories alone and not talk about them to the other children?" An implied threat lay hidden in her words. I knew she was saying that if I didn't, I wouldn't get another chance. It would be a lower floor and electro brain experiments for me.

I nodded, the perfect picture of compliance. I couldn't sneak the flash drive out myself. I couldn't mail it.

Her arm squeezed me tighter one quick last time before she let go and stood up. "Very good. You'll be happy with your decision, Matt. I promise. Yes, the ankle monitor is going to have to stay on for quite a while now, and you will be monitored extremely closely over our security system. But there is no reason you can't fully enjoy yourself on the top floor as long as you behave. All right?"

"Okay." Everything I did on the computer would be monitored second by second, I bet. No sending the contents of the flash drive out electronically. Someone would have to physically carry it out. Coop, Jeffery, and Paige would be watched carefully too. Crud. How was I going to do this?

She paused for a second, her smile wavering ever so slightly. Had she noticed I was carrying something in my pocket? She was going to confiscate the flash drive and then I'd have no hope at all! Was it too late? Maybe I could cover it up with my hand. No. That would be totally obvious.

Honey Lady's smile firmed up as she patted me on

the top of my head, like I was an obedient dog. "You just sit here for one minute while I check to make sure things are back to normal on the top floor."

I could breathe. She hadn't noticed.

She click-clicked over to the heavy industrial doors, pulling out her cell phone.

"Miss Smoot?" The voice of the first-floor girl surprised me. I'd forgotten other people were in the room. "Can I come back to the table now and finish my drawing? There's nothing good on TV."

A First Floor. Two of them actually, counting the boy at the TV.

First Floors remain in this facility only for the short time they spend waiting to be transported to their permanent assignment in a labor-oriented workhouse. A van comes by once a week to pick up any First Floors we've accumulated.

Both the boy and the girl would walk out of here, no questions asked, within the next week. Maybe tomorrow!

Honey Lady stopped talking into her phone to answer the girl. "Um . . . all right, Jessica. But move to that table, over there. Okay?"

With a loud clang Honey Lady walked out the door. Who knew how long she'd be out of the room. One minute? Two? I didn't have long.

252 I chose the girl without hesitating. The boy's eyes

were so glazed over he wouldn't hear a single one of the urgent words I had to say to him.

I hurried over to the far picnic table. "Jessica?"

"Hi! Are you a new First Floor?" Her bright blue eyes sparkled up at me. She couldn't have been more than eleven years old.

"Only for today. Listen, can I borrow your cell phone?" Honey Lady's phone worked on the first floor. It was worth a shot.

"Sure," said Jessica. "As soon as Miss Smoot gives it back, but I think that won't be until I leave for my new workhouse."

Shoot. I should have known. Just how desperate was I to get the flash drive out? Pretty desperate.

"Jessica, I have something really important I need you to do."

"Oh, I'm not allowed to do important things." She bent over her pencil drawing of a horse and a cat dancing in a fountain.

"You're allowed this time. I promise."

Scrunching her nose, she looked up at me. "I'm not very good at things."

Augh! This was killing me. How could I trust such an important mission to someone like her? How did I know she wouldn't turn the flash drive right over to Honey Lady the second I left the first floor?

253

What other choice did I have? This info needed to get out ASAP. The kids on the lower floors couldn't keep being guinea pigs.

"Jessica, listen to me. This won't be hard, I promise, but it's a secret life-and-death mission. You can't tell a single soul in the workhouse. You have to wait until you get out, and then mail this thing I'm going to give you to the newspaper. Do you think you can do that?"

"Mail it?"

Clang! Honey Lady was back. The flash drive still sat in my pocket, and Jessica stared up at me with those huge, uncomprehending eyes.

"Matt, come away from Jessica please."

Cramming both hands into my front pockets, I shrugged. "I was just looking at her picture. She's a really good drawer." I looked down, deep into those eyes. "I stink at drawing. You're the only one I know who can do it."

As Honey Lady click-clicked her way across the room toward us, I bent over the picture, extra low so she couldn't see what I was doing. My hands slipped out of my pockets, and I flicked the flash drive into Jessica's lap.

A hand clamped on my shoulder, nails pressing into my skin through my shirt.

254   "Time to go back to the top floor."

"Okay." I went along with her for a few steps, then turned back and waved. "Good-bye, Jessica. Keep drawing. You're wrong, you know. You're really good. You *can* do important things."

The question was, *would* she do the important thing I had asked her to do?

CHAPTER 24

HOW COULD I BE SO STUPID?
I should be the one on the first floor if I
was dumb enough to hand over every last
bit of evidence that existed to a little girl
who probably had no idea what a flash drive even was.
Ten long days passed on the top floor. I did my schoolwork. I did my paying work. I played paddle-wall-ball
and video games and swam in the pool. Nothing was
fun or challenging or exciting.

I sat in my cubicle, my eyelids drooping as I tried to
answer ambiguous questions about a William Faulkner
short story for my personalized online English class.
How much longer until lunch break? I checked the
clock on my screen. *Groan.* Three and a half more
hours.

And then my screen went blank.

"Hey!"

"Hey!"

"Hey!"

From almost every cubicle.

Coop's head peered around our shared cubie wall. "Your screen black out too, bro?"

I sat there, tapping keys and pushing buttons on the monitor. Nothing. This was really weird. I heard a soft chirpy beep below me, on the ground at the base of my chair. The edge of my jeans rode up an inch as I leaned over to investigate. The dull yellow light on my ankle monitor had gone out. Something in my gut told me it was more than an electrical glitch. I spun a half circle in my chair and stood up to walk over to him. "What do you think's going on?"

"Who cares?" Coop shrugged.

Isaac shuffled out of his cubicle, stretching his arms high over his head. "I'm going back to bed. Somebody get me when the system reboots."

Coop slapped the back of my shoulder. "The gym is calling our names."

"Isaac! You lazy dork. Don't go back to bed!" Kia's head hovered over the wall between her cubicle and Isaac's. He waved her off as he entered the boys' hallway.

"What about water jousting?" asked Jeffery, popping out of his cubie to join me and Coop.

"Naw," said Coop. "The computers could be up and running any time. We'd be all wet and drippy when they called us back."

"Has this happened before?" I asked.

"Never," said Coop.

"Then you really have no idea when—"

"Hey, guys!" Isaac reappeared at the opening to the hallway. "Something's going on outside. I saw it out my window."

Coop, Jeffery, and I looked one another in the eye for half a second before we headed for Isaac.

"Hold up," said Kia, dropping out of sight.

Paige and Madeline huddled together at the end of the girls' cubicles.

"Are you coming?" I asked, reaching out my hand.

Madeline stuck her nose in the air. "Into the boys' rooms? No way."

"Won't we get in trouble?" Paige twisted her fingers together.

"Are you kidding? No one's going to notice with everything else that's going on right now."

She smiled and raced to catch up with us.

After plowing a path through several hundred spaceships and aliens on the floor and shoving Isaac's table to one side, the six of us lined up at his big window.

"It looks like a SWAT team," said Kia. "What in the world would they be doing here?"

My heart thumped hard and fast in my chest. Only one thing I knew of would cause a crackdown on the workhouse. Paige gave my arm a quick squeeze. She thought so too. Somehow that little first-floor girl had gotten our flash drive into the hands of someone who could do something about it. Every nerve in my body tingled. This was it. We'd done it! We'd stopped Honey Lady. She wouldn't be able to hurt the lower-floor kids anymore, and maybe someone would fix the mess she'd made of our accounts.

"Nothing's happening," said Jeffery. My breath caught in the back of my throat. He was right. Something was wrong down there. "They're standing around—they're armed and ready, but no one's coming inside."

"Miss Smoot must be putting up a fight." Coop blurted out a laugh. "Can't you just see her and that receptionist lady hunkered down behind a sofa in the lobby?"

"Maybe the SWAT team will have to laser-blast their way inside," said Isaac, bouncing on his toes at the thought.

I didn't even crack a smile at their jokes.

"I'm going down." I made for the door before the last of my words came out. "I can sneak them inside through the emergency exit, if nothing else."

Kia and Isaac stayed at the window, waiting for the SWAT team to break out the laser guns, I guess. Paige sprinted for her bedroom to retrieve her butane candle lighter and met up with me, Coop, and Jeffery in the elevator hallway a few seconds later. I'd just crumpled a piece of paper and lifted it up for Paige to touch with the flame when we heard the ding of the elevator. *No! Not now when we're only seconds away from slipping into the stairwell!* The click-click of high heels against the hard floor boomed so loudly through the closed space that I wanted to cover my ears.

The clicks stopped, and a gravelly voice spoke. "Just the four people I need."

Crab Woman? She stood at the end of the hallway, her reading glasses swaying from the chain around her neck, holding a—whoa!—gun in her hand. My arms shot straight out at my sides in a wimpy attempt to shield Paige and Jeffery.

"All right, come along," she said.

"Where are we going?" I asked.

"You'll see when we get there. I don't want to hurt anyone, and I won't unless you force me to."

I tried to stall. "But why . . ."

"No more questions. Move!" She twitched the gun, directing us into the elevator.

Obediently, the four of us shuffled inside and huddled together in one corner. Crab Woman took some sort of remote out of her pocket and pressed a button that started our descent. She hadn't said a word.

Coop was silent too, for once in his life. Paige and Jeffery both clung to my arms, trembling enough to register on the Richter scale.

When the doors swooshed open, we found ourselves looking at a much larger space than the hallways we were used to on the other floors.

"Out," said Crab Woman.

Tripping over one another's feet, we moved out of the elevator.

"Basement," said Coop. He had to be right. We walked through a dim space full of exposed pipes and wires lining the unfinished ceiling and walls.

"Stop here." Keeping the gun trained on us, Crab Woman circled around from behind and stepped up to a closed door. She entered a number code into a keypad and held still for an eye scan. The door swished open, and she nodded us through. It turned out to be some sort of windowless storage room, full of electronic equipment. This, at least, was well lit. Before we had the chance to get a good look around us, the door slid shut. Crab Woman settled herself at the one small table and chair in a corner by the door.

"Have a seat," she said. "We're going to be here for a while."

The four of us twisted around, trying to spot another chair or bench or something.

"On the floor," said Crab Woman, flicking a pointed finger toward the far side of the room. "Against that wall. No one's going to get hurt if you just sit there quiet." 261

The room was about the size of one of our bedrooms upstairs. Three long rows of freestanding, open-sided metal shelves full of computers, monitors, and all sorts of other wire-dripping equipment took up much of the space. When we slumped down on the floor, we had a clear view of Crab Woman but were far enough away to be able to talk softly amongst ourselves without her overhearing.

Keeping her eyes on us, she stood up and pulled a laptop off a nearby shelf.

"What do you think is going on?" asked Jeffery.

"This has to be about the flash drive. The SWAT team, the blanking out computers—it's all related." I thunked the back of my head softly and repeatedly against the wall behind me.

"She's in on it with Smoot." Coop spoke quietly to us, then louder to Crab Woman. "Aren't you? You and Smoot are together on this whole scheme."

Crab Woman didn't have to say a word for me to know Coop was right. I should have figured her into my calculations when she brought Honey Lady the wiped laptop that day in the First Floors' room. She probably helped her destroy all the files.

"Who else?" I asked her. "Are the guards in on it too?"

Crab Woman's eyes were focused on her laptop.
"Splitting the money two ways is hard enough. We have

a good security team here—every one of them does exactly what he's told without questions."

"Maybe there's hope," I whispered. "Maybe one of the guards will come down here and find us."

"What would bring one of them down here?" asked Jeffery.

Coop slumped deeper into his slouch on the floor. "Hate to burst your bubble, bro, but I'm not holding my breath for that one."

"Why go to the trouble of locking us down here at all?" asked Paige, her eyes wet. "What's the point?"

None of us could answer.

Crab Woman sat at the table, the gun lying next to the open laptop. We couldn't see the screen, but she had the sound turned up really loud. When my friends and I were quiet, we could hear the audio from the laptop. Interesting that she had wireless Internet down in the basement. The building must have zones, blocking cell phone and unscreened Internet access in all areas where kids might use it and allowing it everywhere else. Crab Woman settled on a news feed, sitting back in her chair and frowning at the screen.

"Kent Kearsley, reporting live from outside the Midwest Federal Debt Rehabilitation Agency work-house," came the slightly crackled-with-static voice from the laptop.

"He's outside, dude," whispered Coop. "Right here. Right now."

The rest of us shushed him. We wanted to listen.

"Shockwaves are still rippling through the country," continued Kent Kearsley, "as the people of this nation ask the question: Are abuses occurring in a place the government billed to us as 'a safe home-away-from-home where children can become a great asset to their families and the community at large'? The answer is still unclear at this time. At this very moment authorities are waiting to gain access to the building and find out whether the children inside are victims—or if some of those very children have played an elaborate hoax on us all."

"Hoax? What is he talking about?"

I shushed Jeffery and leaned forward, straining to catch every one of Kent Kearsley's words.

"As you can imagine, with all the children in residence, authorities are proceeding with extreme caution. The word I've received is that the director of this facility, Sharlene Smoot, will gladly allow them in as soon as she has accounted for and can assure the safety of each and every one of the children under her care."

"Uh, yoo-hoo!" Coop raised one long arm over his head. "I think she missed four of us."

Crab Woman shot him a crusty glare, while I elbowed
him hard in the ribs.

"Quiet! Don't make her mad." Paige's soft words mixed with her muffled sobs.

"While we're waiting, let me recap," said Kent Kearsley. "Twelve-year-old Jessica Richards of Ravenna, Ohio, smuggled allegedly condemning information on a flash drive out of this very workhouse just over one week ago. She then passed the flash drive to Nicole Hopkins—a sales representative for Great Lakes Organics—in the restroom of the Speedy Spot convenience store off Interstate 94. Unaware of what she possessed, Ms. Hopkins let the flash drive sit in her purse until yesterday afternoon, when she took a look at the files. Ms. Hopkins immediately turned the flash drive over to authorities."

Unbelievable. Jessica had handed the flash drive to the first non-FDRA person she met. It could have easily gotten lost or destroyed or forgotten. I couldn't dwell on the huge risk I'd taken by trusting Jessica, because Kent Kearsley wasn't taking a break.

"Now, we have not been informed what specific incriminating evidence the flash drive contains, nor are we clear about the exact nature of the abuses allegedly committed against the children of the Midwest FDRA workhouse. What's more, when first contacted earlier today, Ms. Smoot insisted the contents of the flash drive are fabrications—completely untrue and created by a group of highly intelligent children who live in this facility. As

265

you can see from the security team surrounding the building behind me, authorities are prepared for whichever scenario turns out to be correct. As soon as permission is given, a team will enter the building and begin an inspection of files and interviews with the children in residence."

The turned-off light on my ankle monitor caught my eye. Oh. I got it now. It all made sense.

"No interviewers are going to make it to the basement, are they?" I called across the room to Crab Woman. "Nobody will know we're hidden away down here. We're the only people in the workhouse who know the truth. You're not going to give us the chance to defend ourselves."

The four of us had decided not to tell the other Top Floors the truth about the workhouse until we learned whether the flash drive got out or not. We couldn't see the point in getting Kia, Madeline, and Isaac all angry and excited unless something was actually going to come of it. That had been a mistake. A big one.

"Hey," said Coop, catching on now too. "Miss Smoot is going to convince the good-guy dudes that we're a bunch of punk pranksters, setting out to cause a country-wide jaw-dropper by making up the stuff on that flash drive. That's totally fried, man!"

"Shh!" Paige's mouse voice squeaked with anxiety. "You guys. She has a gun!"

Crab Woman didn't say anything. She just sat, tight-lipped, staring at her computer.

"What are you going to do with us once everyone leaves?" I asked, digging the tips of my fingers into the hard cement floor beneath me. "You won't be able to let us stay in the workhouse, since we'd tell the other kids the truth. You're planning to ship us off somewhere, aren't you—to some juvenile detention center where everyone will think every word we speak is a lie."

"That's not fair!" said Jeffery.

Paige cried more loudly next to me.

"I bet they'll split us up, too," I said. "They'll keep us in solitary confinement for a while, until they break us down so hard we won't dare try to get our story out."

"Dude, that's so twisted!"

"That's the best-case scenario. What do you bet a couple of us never make it to that juvie center?" I was getting so mad, the horror of what I was saying didn't even register. "While we're traveling there, one or more of us will be involved in some sort of tragic accident."

The way Crab Woman sat watching her computer and completely ignoring us made me even angrier.

"No." Paige's soft voice came out surprisingly calm. "All they have to do is force us to stare at the lower-floor computers."

Crab Woman shot a quick glance at us, shifted   267

slightly in her seat, and then refocused her attention on her computer. A wave of ice water gushed through my body. Paige was right. Crab Woman and Honey Lady planned to turn us into living zombies. We'd end up like Brock Reginald.

Looking up at Crab Woman, I slowly shook my head from side to side.

She sneaked another look at us. "Don't worry. Everything is going to turn out just fine."

"Fine for you, maybe!" I yelled. "But what about us?" The muscles in my legs tensed. It was all I could do to keep myself from launching across the room and attacking her.

She'd picked up the gun, though, and held it pointed at us. "Just sit still. Be quiet. All of you!"

Frustration ate me up from the inside. Help stood only a few dozen feet away, on the front lawn of this building, yet we were powerless to do anything other than sit and wait for our brains to get turned into mush.

CHAPTER 25

CRAB WOMAN TURNED BACK TO THE
laptop screen, her fingers remaining
tightly curled around the gun—although
she lowered it to her lap.

She tapped a few buttons to turn up the volume of
Kent Kearsley's voice. "You're with us live as authorities are entering the building. What we're showing you
now is the director of this facility, Sharlene Smoot, as
she is opening the front doors and letting a small group
of investigators inside."

Let the lying begin. Honey Lady could do it too.
She'd sweet-talk the investigators onto her side within
minutes.

"And now the doors slide shut," said Kent Kearsley.
"We will keep you informed of any further developments the instant they happen."

Long minutes ticked away with no new reported
developments. Crab Woman continued to watch, her
eyes beginning to glaze over and her mouth stretching
into a wide yawn every so often. Coop shoulder-nudged

me. We sat silently, watching as her head sank forward and then jerked back up fast. Clearing her throat, Crab Woman adjusted herself to sit up straight in her chair. With the gun lying across her thighs, she turned to the laptop. She must have brought up some sort of card game, because she kept mouthing words like "red ace" and "black seven."

The game couldn't have been much of a challenge. Her eyes began to droop. *Fall asleep! Come on!* Her head slid forward until her chin rested on her chest. I rolled onto the balls of my feet, in a crouch, ready to spring across the room and knock that gun out of her lap. Crab Woman's head jerked up again. Still holding the gun, she popped out of the chair, shaking her head and wiggling her arms. In one sharp movement she turned to the shelves of overflow technology. Her eyes scanned them and fixed on a box on a middle shelf. A wide smile spread across her face. She reached into the box and brought out a squat tube with a mouthpiece, just like an asthma inhaler except . . . *Oh, no. Not that!* She pressed a few buttons, adjusting the dosage, brought the tube to her mouth, and sucked in a deep breath. It was a caffeine inhaler. I sank back down the couple of inches to the floor. Figures the workhouse would keep a supply of caffeine inhalers on-site. I didn't think any of the adults here ever slept.

Crab Woman stretched and smiled even more broadly. She'd never fall asleep now. We had about two minutes before the caffeine kicked in. Two minutes before she became so totally aware and alert that we'd never be able to pull anything over on her.

"Paige," I whispered. "Go tell her you need to use the bathroom. Make it sound like an emergency."

"She's got a gun!" Paige's wobbly voice whispered back.

"No, look. She just set it down on the table. Start talking before you even get up. But get close to her. Just do it. You'll be fine."

Without questioning me further, Paige rose to her feet, using my shoulder to push herself up.

"Excuse me?" said Paige, barely loud enough for Crab Woman to hear. "I hate to bother you, but I really need a restroom."

Coop spoke close to my ear. "What's up, bro?"

"We're the kings of the distraction technique. Remember?" I got my legs under me.

Crab Woman watched Paige closely as she inched toward the little table in the corner. "You can hold it," her gravelly voice said.

"No, I can't," said Paige.

"What's the plan?" asked Jeffery.

"There is no plan," I whispered. "We're just going to go."

"Sit back down," said Crab Woman to Paige. Without getting up Coop, Jeffery, and I slid toward the shelves.

"You don't understand." Paige stood within a few feet of Crab Woman now, crossing her legs and bouncing up and down. "I drank three big cups of orange juice for breakfast."

Paige was a good actress. I found myself feeling bad for her.

Crab Woman's lips crinkled. I could tell she was perplexed. She couldn't let Paige out, but she also didn't want a smelly mess locked up with us in this storage room for who knew how many more hours. Crab Woman's attention was completely focused on Paige. That made us boys invisible. Staying as low to the floor as possible, Coop, Jeffery, and I darted around the first row of shelves. We crawled toward the other end of the room, where Paige stood with Crab Woman. At the end of the row, we slowly climbed to our feet. Coop carefully pulled a long green extension cord off a shelf, flashing me his goofy smile as he unwound it in his hands.

"Please! I'll only be a minute." Paige sounded desperate. "I'll come right back. I promise. You can even come with me, if you want."

"I can't leave the others . . . hey!" Crab Woman had noticed. She'd probably looked to where we'd been sitting when she mentioned us. We jumped on the fleeting moment of surprise. Jeffery reached through the open shelf and pushed a clunky monitor off the other side. Crab Woman screeched as shattered glass skittered across the floor. Coop and I sprang out from around the end of the shelf in time to see Paige knock the gun across the table an instant before Crab Woman grabbed it. Paige let out little *erp*s and squeals as she pushed the gun as far from Crab Woman as possible, first with her hand and then across the floor with her foot.

At the exact moment Crab Woman began to spring from her chair, I shoved her back into it, hard. Coop was quick to wrap the extension cord tight around her upper body. Jeffery pushed a couple more monitors off the shelf for good measure. One of them smashed down on top of the gun.

Jeffery's face peered out from behind the far end of the row of shelves in time to see Coop and me tie off the cord. A smile jumped on his face, and he crossed the room to join the rest of us. "Now what?"

Paige tried the door handle. "We're still locked in."

"And you'll *stay* locked in." Crab Woman's voice snapped.

"She opened it with an eye scan," I said.

Instantly Crab Woman clamped her eyes tightly shut.

"Better tie down her legs, too," said Coop. "I don't want to get kicked."

273

"Just stay back from her," said Jeffery.

"We can't," said Paige. She bent down to hold one of Crab Woman's legs tight to the chair. I held the other one, and Coop secured her with another long extension cord.

"Ready?" I asked Coop as I grabbed the chair underneath the seat.

"Let me help!" said Jeffery, stepping behind the chair. "We're forcing her to get the eye scan, huh? Cool! But she entered a code into the keypad first."

"I've got it," said Paige. Good thing most Top Floors have amazing memories. Paige punched the code into the keypad as the guys and I lifted Crab Woman and her chair off the floor. Her mouth was squeezed as tightly closed as her eyes, but little protesting sounds still leaked out of her.

Grunting, we carried the chair a couple of feet to the scanner by the door.

"Up!" I said.

Bending our knees, we strained and got her eyes to the right height, grateful Crab Woman wasn't very big.

"Paige!" I called. "Hurry!"

Paige reached around Coop and pried Crab Woman's eye open, holding it long enough for the laser to scan it. *Swoosh.*

The door opened. Freedom.

• • •

Crab Woman's screams chased us until we closed the door to the emergency stairs. Our running footsteps boomed like thunder in the stairwell.

A man in a dark suit stood by Crab Woman's desk, and another one sat working at her computer.

"We know the truth!" I yelled before we had even crossed the lobby. "The flash drive is real!"

The standing man narrowed his eyes, looking hard at us. "Who are you? What do you know about the flash drive?"

"We're the ones who found the information. We made the download and smuggled it out." He had to believe us. *Please—everyone can't already be totally brainwashed by Honey Lady's lies.*

"You four made the flash drive?" he asked.

"Yes!" we all yelled at the same time.

"Hold on one second." He lifted a two-way communication device to his mouth. "Peterson? Chault here. Yeah, I've got four kids with me who claim they're responsible for the flash drive."

A static-laced voice answered over the device. "Four? Three boys and a girl?"

"Affirmative."

"That's odd." The speaker didn't click off, but he was no longer talking to our lobby man. "Sharlene, come over for a moment, please." We heard some mumbled, laughing voices in the background. Honey Lady had schmoozed them all good. They were all on a friendly, first-name basis now, by the sound of it. Every last agent in this building had turned to cookie dough in her hands. "I thought you said the four in question were unavailable for interviews. You said they'd escaped early this morning and run away. We have a team out searching the city for them."

Our lobby agent spoke. "Do you want me to send them back to Sharlene's office?"

"Wait. I'll come get them." The transmission cut out. A few minutes later Agent Peterson walked out of the hall behind Crab Woman's desk. With a sharp twitch of his hand he signaled us to follow him.

Half a dozen agents were wandering around the massive office Agent Peterson escorted us into.

"Where's Honey Lady?" I asked.

Coop jabbed me in the side. "Smoot."

"Where's Miss Smoot?"

Peterson did a quick scan of the room. "Yes, where is Sharlene?"

"I thought she went with you," said a female agent.

"No," said Peterson. "Odd that she'd disappear right when I need her to confront our four key witnesses—in fact, now that I think about it, how did you four get inside? We have the perimeter of this building secured, and I haven't received a report of anyone trying to get in."

"We never left!" I said. "We were being held hostage, hidden away in the basement. She didn't want us to talk to you."

"But why—if you are the pranksters, I'd think she'd want to see you punished. Unless . . ."

"Unless we're telling the truth. The evidence on the flash drive is real!"

Peterson turned to another agent. "Find Smoot. Bring her back here. Now!"

The second agent nodded. "We'll find her. It's not like she can go anywhere. Like you just said, we've got the building surrounded."

"Where does she think she can hide?" said Peterson. "Stupid of her to try."

I noticed Jeffery edge his way behind the big desk in the middle of the room. He pulled out a drawer and rummaged inside before moving on to the next drawer. If one of the agents noticed, he could get in trouble. I tried to catch his eye, to signal him to knock it off, but he never looked up.

I eased over to the desk. "Jeffery, what are you doing?"

"I'm looking for my keys. I don't want them to get confiscated when this room is sealed off as evidence."

"Keys?"

"My PMC. Remember? Miss Smoot wouldn't let me keep my own keys."

Jeffery and I locked eyes over the desk.

"Your PMC."

"She's going to steal it!" said Jeffery.

I turned fast to Agent Peterson. "She's going to the roof. There's a Personal Mini Copter up there!"

You'd have thought a bomb was about to go off under Honey Lady's desk the way the agents tore out of that office. I followed. They all sprinted for the back set of emergency stairs. That would take way too long. I bolted through the lobby to the elevator and pushed the button to open it.

"Matthew Dunston!" I yelled before the doors even slid shut. Within a few seconds I arrived on the top floor, zipped out of the elevator, and dashed into the stairwell. I ran up the stairs three at a time and burst through the rooftop door.

Honey Lady stood inside a fenced-off tennis court next to the skylights from the top floor. Jeffery's PMC sat in the middle of the brand-new, never-been-used, didn't-even-have-a-net-up tennis court. I gave my head a shake. Kids in other workhouses got to play in their rooftop tennis courts, but not us. No. In order for us to do that, we'd have to have access to the stairs, and if we had access to the stairs, we'd be able to go to other floors.

Honey Lady wasn't having any of that in *her* workhouse.

The court was located next to the skylights, as close to the center of the roof as possible—probably to help keep any wild balls that made it over the top of the fence from falling off the building. The location would make the PMC very difficult to see from the ground—which is why its existence had been a surprise to the agents.

"Hey!" I yelled, running toward the court. Looking up at me, Honey Lady pinched the padlock on the gate closed, shutting me out. She sprinted toward the helicopter. The fence stretched tall above me—to contain those stray balls—but the openings between the chain links were big enough for my feet to slip into easily. I'd made it to the top before the agents slammed through the second doorway on the other side of the roof. Honey Lady dropped Jeffery's keys on the ground and stopped to pick them up. She glanced at me and, with a little squeal, lunged into the PMC. I practically slid down the fence and into the court. Her frantic squeaks continued as she strapped herself into the one seat of the little helicopter.

Three male agents simultaneously tried to climb the fence, but their big shoes kept slipping out of the links, and none of them could make it more than a few feet off the ground. A fourth agent tried to break the lock on the gate with his bare hands.

The blades of the copter started whirling.

"Stop!" I yelled. Honey Lady probably couldn't even hear me anymore—not that it would have made a difference. How could I stop her? Her eyes darted back and forth as she studied the controls. As far as I knew, PMCs were fairly simple to operate. She'd be in the air in no time.

A female agent arrived and with her smaller feet quickly climbed the fence. If I could just hold Honey Lady here for a minute or two longer . . . I noticed a big plastic storage box sitting next to a bench by the fence. There had to be tennis rackets inside. I yanked open the box. I could take a racket, jam it between the helicopter blades—and rip my arm off in the process. Hey! There were basketballs inside the box too. With a quick glance I noticed the hoops on either end of the court.

Basketballs.

The opening of that helicopter should be much easier to shoot through than a hoop.

Come on, Matt, an easy shot.

Honey Lady let out a little scream, wincing at the approaching ball. I missed, banging the top of the copter to the side of the opening.

Twelve divided by four equals three.

I shot again, Honey Lady squealed again. Another miss. I was down to .75.

The storage box didn't hold too many more balls. Honey Lady sat up straight; she was finished fiddling with the instrument panel. Her fingers curled around the steering stick.

I grabbed another ball. *Make it more like a hard pass than a shot—it's not that high.* Honey Lady shrieked, ducking sideways as the ball slammed into her shoulder. Yes! I was up to 6! Or 3.75 if I used Lester's calculating system and 2.625 if I used Brennan's.

I fired off a few more shots, keeping Honey Lady distracted and unbalanced—and out of the air. With a grunt, the agent swung her leg over the top of the fence.

"Hurry!" I yelled. "I'm on my last basketball."

The entire fence shuddered as she made her hasty, half-falling descent. My last ball flew through the air, and the agent followed it fast in a crouching run. She grabbed Honey Lady's shoulder, unbuckled the straps, and yanked her out of the helicopter before she'd recovered from her last hit from the ball.

I slumped down on the bench, resting my head in my hands, my fingers threading into my hair.

Breathe. You can breathe now.

Long minutes passed. Short Gorilla Guard arrived and cut through the lock. Several agents walked Honey Lady past me. I sat up tall. Little frizzes of hair stuck out all over her head. Her eyes looked red and puffy, and her usual smooth confidence was nowhere to be seen.

She shot a hot glare in my direction.

"You can't be mad at me," I said, shrugging. "I was only following your instructions. You're the one who told me to go ahead and try to get the story out."

Her mouth dropped open, and she sputtered out a few incoherent words as the agents pulled her off of the court.

Bye, Honey Lady.

JEFFERY AND I WERE SITTING IN THE cushy chairs in the lobby of the FDRA workhouse. Seven months had passed since I'd first come to live here.

"Isn't Lauren supposed to come down?" he asked.

"She won't miss this," I said, my fingers drumming out a fast beat on the armrest. She'd die if she didn't get here in time. "Look, there's Paige!"

As she walked down the short hallway from the elevator, Paige wore a smile so bright it would have glowed in the dark. She waved at me, but her real smile was for the people sitting in the chairs across from Jeffery and me. They sprang to their feet when they saw her.

Paige dropped her duffel bag and ran and jumped into their arms. They all hugged and cried and hugged some more.

"Good, I didn't miss it," said Lauren as she ran up behind me. "I forgot I had vacuuming duty. I was afraid I wouldn't get to say good-bye."

"Naw, Paige wouldn't have left without a slobbery hug from her best friend." I jabbed her in the ribs as she stood leaning against my chair.

"I don't know," said Lauren. "I think she's forgotten all about this place already."

She hadn't. Within a few minutes Paige let go of her parents. Her dad picked up the duffel bag and slung it over his shoulder. Her mom still held on to Paige's hands, but eventually she let go and allowed her to walk over to us. Jeffery and I stood up. Lauren ran forward and hugged her.

"Bye, Paige. I'll miss you," she said.

"I'll miss you, too," said Paige. Bouncing on the balls of her feet, she turned to Jeffery and me. "Good-bye, you guys. I can't believe it. I'm going home!"

"You deserve it," I said. "You worked really hard."

"I never would've made it out of here without you two." She gave Jeffery a short, stooped hug. "Thank you." She let go of him and grabbed me tight around the neck. "Thank you, Matt. I'm never going to forget you." She started to let go, but paused and whispered, "I liked the kiss."

And then she whirled away. Her words had come out so soft and fast it took me a moment to process them. By that time Paige was back with her parents, walking toward the reception desk where Crab Woman used to sit. My cheeks burned, and I felt a lurch inside my stomach. That kiss had been pretty great. I hoped Paige remembered to e-mail me. She'd promised she would. How soon would it come? That night?

Lauren, Jeffery, and I watched from a distance as Paige's parents signed some forms. Mrs. Marcus, the woman who had taken over Crab Woman's job, talked them through the process. Just like checking out of a hotel. We waved one last time as Paige and her parents walked out the front door.

"Lauren, sweetie, come on over here and get a piece of gum."

"Okay!" Lauren skipped to Mrs. Marcus's desk and plucked a bright round gumball out of a crystal dish. Mrs. Marcus had more energy than Nana did, even though she seemed a little older.

"What about you, Matt, Jeffery?"

I waved her off. "I'm okay."

"It's shaping up to be a beautiful fall day. You kids planning on playing outside?"

"Sure. Maybe," I said. "Later, during lunch break."

"Go up to the roof, and I'll take you on in a game of HORSE."

I had to laugh. "You're on." Mrs. Marcus could probably beat Brennan or Lester if they had been here, but she'd have to work hard to get the better of me—

especially now that I didn't have an ankle monitor weighing me down anymore.

"Hey, Matt!" Brock Reginald and Gorilla Man walked down the hall behind the reception desk toward us. Now that he wasn't subjected to constant doses of electro-info-dumping, Brock had turned back into a normal human being. He no longer had the brains of a Top Floor, but—from what I gathered—he was at about a fourth-floor level and had found his calling working with the security guards. He'd been redesigning their monitoring systems, and my guess was there was no way I'd be able to cause another blackout of the system again—not that I needed to.

"Brock, bud, how's it going?"

"Good."

"Keeping us safe?"

"You bet!"

Gorilla Man nodded at me as he and Brock passed. "Matt."

"Hey, Mr. G." Turned out Gorilla Man's last name was Gillia. Did I have him pegged or what?

"Come on," I said to Lauren and Jeffery. "Let's get back to our floors. School hours are about to start."

The elevator took us up to the second floor. Lauren and I got out.

"You guys want to come up for swimming after dinner tonight?" Jeffery asked.

"Sure," said Lauren.

"It will have to wait until after an hour of paddle-wall-ball," I said. "Coop would burst a couple of blood vessels if we missed his turn in the gym. He's been waiting for weeks."

"Okay. See you later."

Lauren stared at the elevator for a few seconds after the doors closed. "Sometimes I think it would be nice not to care about how much you spend. I'd like to live on the top floor and have one of those nice rooms all to myself."

"It's not worth it," I said, wrapping an arm around her and leading her into the big main room of the second floor. "Trust me."

We split off to go to our own computer stations. Sliding into my chair, I turned my computer on and smiled at the guys sitting on either side of me. Forget about privacy on the second floor; a little more elbow room would be nice. I can't complain about my computer, though. I was able to bring it down with me from the top floor. Second-floor computers—at least the ones here now—are made to handle basic tasks, like data entry and word processing—not the complicated math modeling work I do. Continuing to pull in top-floor money while living on the second floor is part of the arrangement I negotiated with the new workhouse supervisors.

Otherwise I'd never be able to dig myself out of the debt I created. Spending a couple of days at online auctions selling off all the junk I bought in that one weak moment helped a little too.

Glancing around the rows of tables and computers, I saw Lauren across the room, already deeply concentrating on her monitor. Paige's old top-floor computer now sat empty next to her. About a dozen computers from upper floors were mixed in with the fifty or so second-floor computers.

The workhouse is all about choice now. Since the rules eased up considerably regarding who can go where in the building, living on the second floor isn't so bad. The pool is jam-packed every day, and you have to sign up weeks in advance to get an hour in the paddle-wall-ball court. But it's only fair. The biggest downside is having to sleep in a bunk bed on a lumpy mattress in a long dorm-type room with thirty other guys. Before I came to the workhouse, I would have been ashamed of living the way I do now—it's certainly nothing to brag about. The weird thing is, once I get out of here, I'm not going to leave the details of the living conditions out of the story when I tell it to Brennan and Lester and whoever else wants to listen.

A soft ping signaled me that I had a new e-mail.
Lauren and I caught eyes through the jumble of kids

and computers. It was from Mom and Dad. Lauren had gotten it too.

Dear Matt and Lauren,

I'm so nervous! I start my new job today. Do you think anyone will listen to my ideas at the boutique? I certainly know the store well enough—I've spent enough money there over the years. It's only part-time, so I can still try to squeeze the supplement business an hour or two a day and see if I can get anything out of it. So far it's been a dry sponge, but I can't give up quite yet. I've got to run! I have no idea what I'm going to wear. I was good and didn't buy a new outfit for today, so I've got to scrounge up something respectable out of my old rags. LOL ☺
Love and love and love!!!
Mom

Hey, guys,

Don't let Mom fool you. She's so confident and excited I can barely keep her feet touching the ground. You two hanging in there? We'll have you home before you know it. We sure do miss you. Golf season is ending too soon! I'm taking a potential client out today. Nothing big. It will

take five clients like him to make up for one
Dupree—it's been months. Can you tell it still
gets me that I didn't nail that one? Just like
fishing—you always go on and on about the one
that got away. I've got to get going now myself.
Nana has a big stack of pancakes on the
table, ready for Abbie and me to dig in. I want
to get to them while they're still hot. It's great
having Nana here, even though I go through
antihistamines like they were popcorn to keep
my allergic reactions to Dear Sweet Buffy ;-)
under control. We'll figure something out so
you can have your room back once you get out,
Matt. We'll make it happen. I promise.
Dad

It's going to take a while, but my family is getting
there. We have a huge mountain of debt we have to dig
out from under, but if we all try our best, we should be
able to keep Abbie from having to come to the workhouse. I most likely won't get out until I turn eighteen,
and I'm learning to accept—or at least deal—with that. I
hope to do better for Lauren.

A shaggy blond head popped up over the top-floor
computer on the table across from me.

"Today's the day, bro! Paddle-wall-ball!"

"I'm going to smash you this time, Coop."

"In your dreams, dude."

Hardly. Of all the things I fantasize about, winning at paddle-wall-ball is not even in the top one hundred. I dream about going to college—and doing it on a sweet scholarship so my personal account will remain debt-free—and traveling around the world, far away from this workhouse, and sitting down to dinner with my entire family. Mom will make meat loaf.

It will happen—all of it. Eventually. For now I've decided to be happy with the life I have, even though it's not the life I thought I'd have a year ago. I'm making the best of things. I'm smart. Smart enough to be a Top Floor, even though I choose not to be one. The possibilities the future holds for me are limitless.